VOLUME SEVEN:
THE ONCE AND FUTURE KING

FIRST PRINTING: FEBRUARY 2020

ISBN: 978-1-5343-1466-5

RYAN FERRIER
story and lettering

PRISCILLA PETRAITES
art

MARCO LESKO
colors

TIM DANIEL
frame

IMAGE COMICS, INC.
Robert Kirkman—Chief Operating Officer
Erik Larsen—Chief Financial Officer
Todd McFarlane—President
Marc Silvestri—Chief Executive Officer
Jim Valentino—Vice President
Eric Stephenson—Publisher/Chief Creative Officer
Jeff Boison—Director of Publishing Planning & Book Trade Sales
Chris Ross—Director of Digital Services
Jeff Stang—Director of Direct Market Sales
Kat Salazar—Director of PR & Marketing
Drew Gill—Cover Editor
Heather Doornink—Production Director
Nicole Lapalme—Controller
IMAGECOMICS.COM

MELANIE HACKETT
edits

MARC LOMBARDI
communications

JIM VALENTINO
publisher/book design

RAT QUEENS created by KURTIS J. WIEBE and ROC UPCHURCH

A

SWAMP ROMP SPECIAL

ALL RIGHT, MY SWEET FUCKLES-- *DRINKS!*

THANKS, HANNAH! YOU'RE A DOLL. NEXT ROUND'S ON BRAGA.
BUT--
HUH? OH. YOU THOUGHT... IN THIS ECONOMY? NO, THESE ARE *MINE*, BETTY.

HRMPH I'M BROKE, AND THIS WENCH STILL NEEDS QUENCHED.
I'VE NEVER MET A SMIDGEN, LET ALONE A TROLL, THAT COULD THROW THEM DOWN LIKE YOU. I THINK YOU'VE HAD MORE THAN ENOUGH.
AGREED. I'M SHATTERED, DEE.
WE HAVEN'T HAD A DECENT PAYING QUEST SINCE MAESTRO MADE US SETTLE OUR TABS.

I HAVE A THIRST!
THAT'S MINE, YOU SNEAKY FUCK-STICK!
EVOKAR--
HANNAH, NO--
AH-HEH-HEH-HEM!

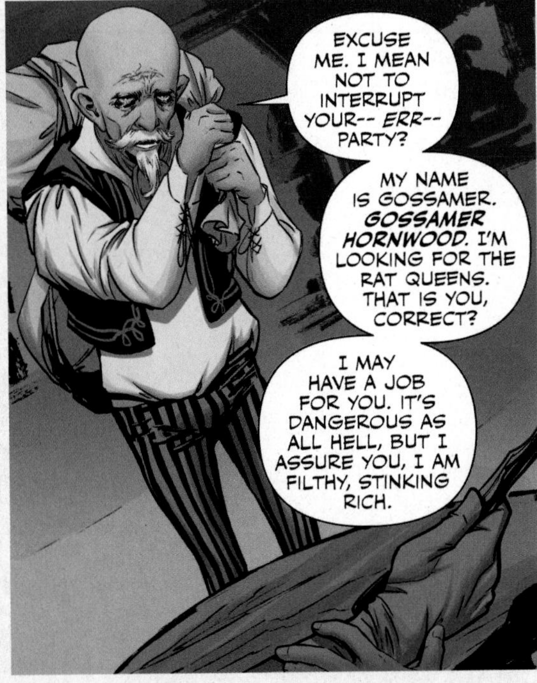
EXCUSE ME. I MEAN NOT TO INTERRUPT YOUR-- *ERR*-- PARTY?
MY NAME IS GOSSAMER. *GOSSAMER HORNWOOD.* I'M LOOKING FOR THE RAT QUEENS. THAT IS YOU, CORRECT?
I MAY HAVE A JOB FOR YOU. IT'S DANGEROUS AS ALL HELL, BUT I ASSURE YOU, I AM FILTHY, STINKING RICH.

NEXT ROUND'S ON GOSSIPER HORNYMAN!
NO OFFENSE, SIR, BUT WE CAN'T JUST TAKE ANY JOB THAT COMES OUR WAY FROM SICKLY OLD MEN. WE'RE A *BOUTIQUE* BAND OF ROGUES FOR HIRE.
DEE, ZIP IT.
WHAT KIND OF DEAL ARE WE TALKING HERE, MR. HORNWOOD?

THIS DEAL. *REVENGE*, AS IT WERE.
WHOA, IS THAT...
NO WAY.
OH. MY. GODS!

MY CHAUNCEY. OH, MY BELOVED, BEAUTIFUL CHAUNCEY. AS YOU CAN SEE, HE'S A LITTLE WORSE FOR WEAR, BUT HE WAS MY CHERISHED STEED.

HELP THIS FORLORN HEART O' MINE HEAL, I BEG YOU. BRING ME THE HEAD OF THE DERANGED BEAST THAT TORE MY CHAUNCEY'S HEAD FROM HUSK...

...AND THE ENTIRETY OF MY VAST FORTUNE WILL BE YOURS. IT MAY COME TO SURPRISE YOU THAT I AM SOON TO BE REUNITED WITH MY CHAUNCEY.
SOON, I WILL BE DEAD FROM AN UNTREATABLE, UNKNOWN DISEASE-- BUT NO ONE TO LEAVE THE SPOILS OF MY LUCKY, LOVE-FILLED LIFE.

I HAVEN'T SEEN AN *ACTUAL* UNICORN SINCE I WAS A BABY! MY MOM DID DO A BUTT-TON OF MUSHROOMS THOUGH...
UGH, GET THAT NASTY THING OFF THE TABLE. I DON'T SEE THE BIG DEAL. UNICORNS. WHOOPITY-FUCKIN'-DOO.
PRETTY BABE...SUCH A PRETTY HORNED BABE.

"VAST FORTUNE," WE'VE HEARD THAT ONE BEFORE. SO TELL US, THIS BEAST THAT KILLED YOUR UNICORN--WHO, WHAT, AND WHERE ARE WE TALKING, EXACTLY?
YES, WELL, SEE, THAT'S THE TRICKY THING...

MY CHAUNCEY WAS... SEPARATED FROM BODY... IN MY SUMMER HOME. DON'T LET THE NAME NOR REPUTATION FOOL YOU, IT CAN BE QUITE LOVELY UNDER MOONLIGHT.
THE SWAMPS OF ***GNARNATHAL FOREST.***

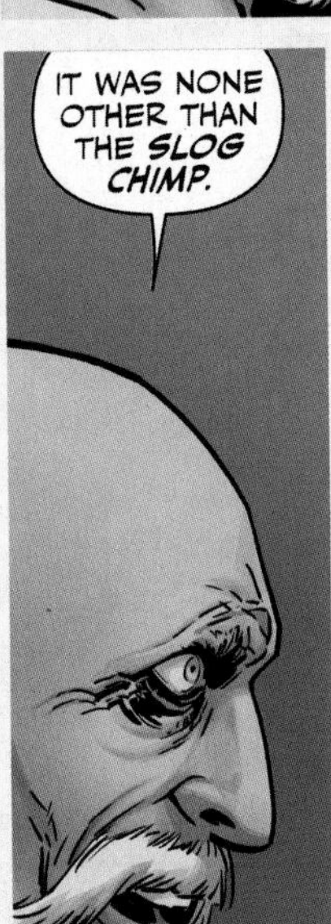
IT WAS NONE OTHER THAN THE ***SLOG CHIMP.***

WELL, NEVER MIND. HE'S NUTS.
YES! WE'LL DO IT!

NO. NO NO NO. NOPE. FUCKIN' ***NOPE,*** BETTY.

WELL, THIS JUST GOT INTERESTING, AT LEAST.

OKAY, BUT CAN WE KEEP THE SWEET UNICORN BABE?

WE'RE NOT ACTUALLY GOING TO CONSIDER THIS. THE SLOG CHIMP ISN'T REAL. EVERYONE KNOWS THAT. IT'S AN ***URBAN LEGEND.***
WHAT? NO IT ISN'T! I'VE SEEN IT!
BULLSHIT. YOU HAVEN'T SEEN ANYTHING, YOU WERE HIGH. ALSO, FUCK THAT. I NEVER WANT TO SEE OR HEAR OR THINK ABOUT THAT THING.
LOOK AT HIM, HE'S LOST HIS MARBLES. IT WAS PROBABLY JUST A HUNGRY TRASH-SMIDGEN.

LET'S JUST PUT IT TO A VOTE--YEA OR NAY FOR HORNWOOD'S QUEST?
I ***KNOW*** THE SLOG CHIMP. I SWEAR! LET'S DO IT.
WE NEED THE MONEY. HELL, WE NEED THE ***CHANCE*** OF MONEY.
NO. NUH-UH. NO WAY.
FINE, BUT THE HEAD STAYS WITH ME.

I CAN'T BELIEVE WE'RE DOING THIS. WE'VE BEEN ON SOME DUMB QUESTS BEFORE, SURE--BUT THE SLOG CHIMP?
INDULGE ME IN A MILLION TOLD-YOU-SO'S WHEN WE GET LOST IN A SWAMP WITH NO REWARD.
YE HAVE LITTLE FAITH, BRAGA. YOU'LL SEE.
SHE'S RIGHT, BETTY. IT'S JUST A TERRIFYING, HORRIBLE BED-TIME STORY.

"TOLD TO KIDS TO MAKE THEM PISS THEMSELVES INTO OBEDIENCE WHEN THEIR SWINGER PARENTS ARE HOSTING A 'GROWN UPS PARTY.'"
"'HANNAH VIZARI, YOU GO TO SLEEP AND STAY ASLEEP...LEST YOU WANT THE SLOG CHIMP TO TEAR EVERY GRISTLE OF MEAT FROM YOUR LITTLE, WEAK BONES!'"

AW, IS SOMEONE STILL A WIDDLE SCARED OF THE MYSTEEERIOUS SLOG CHIMP FROM THE SWAMPS OF GNARNATHAL?
DEE. I DON'T BELIEVE IN THAT STUFF. THAT'S CRAZY. NOT REAL.
GODS, PLEASE, PLEASE DON'T BE REAL.

I DON'T KNOW HOW I ENDED UP IN A BOG OF ALL PLACES, BUT SURE ENOUGH, THE SLOG CHIMP SHOWED UP. ONE OF THE FUNNEST NIGHTS OF MY LIFE. I THINK.
HEY. YOU FEELING OKAY, VIOLET? YOU LOOK KINDA ≶BLERG≶
HM? OH. YEAH. JUST A LITTLE TIRED STILL. MUST BE THE SWAMP AIR.
DO YOU THINK WE'LL SEE A LIVE UNICORN? I'VE WANTED ONE *FOREVER*.

BEAUTIFUL, BRILLIANT CREATURES, AREN'T THEY? JUST MAJESTIC.
THEY GIVE SO MUCH LOVE TO THEIR MASTER. TAKE LOVE, TOO. BOTH WAYS. FOREVER.

OHHH SLOGGGG-YYY? SLOGGY! WHERE YOU AT, MY FRIEND?
BETTY! SHUT YOUR SMIDGEY LITTLE TRASH HOLE!
IF THIS THING IS REAL-- IT'S NOT--WE NEED TO SNEAK UP ON IT. SLICE ITS NECK OPEN WHILE IT SLEEPS. BLEED THE SUCKER OUT BEFORE IT DOES HORRIBLE THINGS TO US.

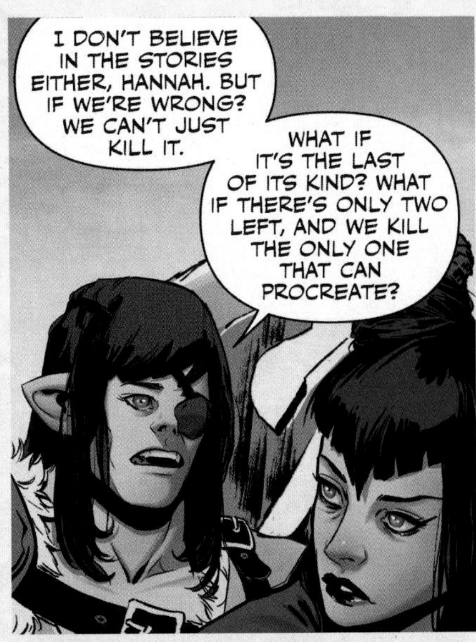
I DON'T BELIEVE IN THE STORIES EITHER, HANNAH. BUT IF WE'RE WRONG? WE CAN'T JUST KILL IT.
WHAT IF IT'S THE LAST OF ITS KIND? WHAT IF THERE'S ONLY TWO LEFT, AND WE KILL THE ONLY ONE THAT CAN PROCREATE?

I'M ALL FOR KILLING, OBVIOUSLY. BUT GENOCIDE? I'D LIKE TO STILL SLEEP AT NIGHT, THANK YOU.

I DON'T KNOW, BRAGA--IMAGINE THE COIN A FREAKING TAXIDERMIED SLOG CHIMP COULD PULL IN PALISADE. OL' BURNEY STILL SELLS OUT OF SLOGGY SHIRTS AND STUFFIES EVERY SPRING.
ON THE OTHER HAND... A REAL, LIVE, IN-THE-FLESH URBAN LEGEND?

WE'LL BE RICH.
I'LL KILL IT FOR FREE.
YOU GUYYYS, HE'S NOT THAT BAD!
HRMM

BY THE SMELL OF THINGS, THIS IS IT--THE SWAMPS OF GNARNATHAL FOREST. KEEP YOUR WITS ABOUT YOU.
OH GOOD, GREAT, WONNNDERFUL. NOW I CAN JUST KEEP CONTINUALLY SHITTING AND NONE OF YOU WILL EVER KNOW.
WE HAVE TO ASSUME THE CREATURE IS REAL. AND REMEMBER, WE KNOW LITERALLY NOTHING ABOUT IT.

KOFF KAFF!
HOH THERE, MS. RED QUEEN... YOU-YOU'VE HAD MY CHAUNCEY THIS WHOLE JOURNEY... I MISS MY STEED.
MIGHT I...PLEASE... HAVE MY SWEET, SWEET BOY BACK?

KOFF HANDS OFF. I'M NNG IN CHARGE OF THE UNICORN ON THIS KAFF QUEST.
GODS, ONCE YOU BREAK KOFF THROUGH THE ROTTEN MEAT IT SMELLS LIKE GUHH LAVENDER AND CUPCAKES.

OH, CHAUNCEY. MY BEAUTIFUL, WARM, SOFT BOY. I MISSED YOU SO!
HRRRGL

EASY, VI. TAKE IT EASY!
THAT WAS SSOOO GROSS. AWESOME.
BETTY!
IS SHE OKAY, DEE? THAT DOESN'T LOOK LIKE JUST SWAMP AIR--SHE LOOKS AS GNARLY AS THE OLD MAN.

I DON'T KNOW. I'VE NEVER SEEN THIS MANY--ACTUALLY, EVERY SYMPTOM ALL AT ONCE BEFORE. I'M NOT ACTUALLY SURE WHAT'S WRONG.
I'LL CAST A PAIN RELIEF SPELL, BUT I CAN'T HEAL HER UNLESS I KNOW THE SOURCE. MAYBE WE SHOULD HEAD BACK...

GO BACK? OH NO NO NO, YOU'RE SO CLOSE. AND, WHY, MY FORTUNE IS BURIED RIGHT IN THESE SWAMPS, SO IT BEHOOVES YOU TO STAY AND COMPLETE THIS JOB.

HOLD UP, HORSE-FUCKER... DID YOU SAY "BURIED"?
OOH, IT'S LIKE A TREASURE HUNT! WITH NO MAP!
'KAY. LET'S KILL HIM.

HERE'S HOW THIS IS GOING TO WORK, HORNWOOD. YOU'RE STAYING RIGHT HERE WITH VIOLET WHILE WE TAKE CARE OF YOUR ≈GUHH≈ MYSTERY CHIMP.
IF WE COME BACK AND YOU'RE NOT HERE WITH VIOLET--AND IF SO MUCH AS A HAIR ON HER HEAD OR FACE IS OUT OF PLACE...

...I'M GOING TO ZAP YOUR SHRIVELED LITTLE UNICORN-STUFFING COCK OFF AND USE IT TO MAKE VIGOROUS LOVE TO EACH OF YOUR EYE SOCKETS.

⩨SNFF SNFF⩨
WHOA-- YOU GALS SMELL WHAT I'M SMELLIN'?
YEAH, THIS PLACE REEKS LIKE THE INSIDE OF N'RYGOTH'S BUTTHOLE.
SNIFF A LI'L DEEPER, BRAGA.
IT'S...MMM... LAVENDER? OH! AND--

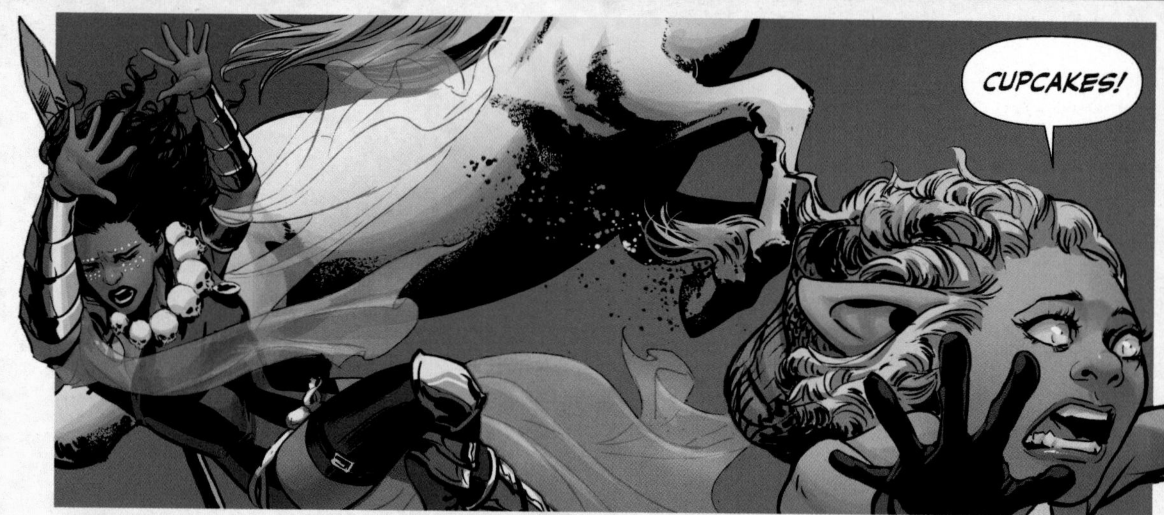

CUPCAKES!

HUFFFF
HOLY FUCK-NUGGETS-- A UNICORN! AN ACTUAL, REAL, LIVE UNICORN!
AWW, IT'S SOOO CUTE!
I DON'T KNOW, IT LOOKS KIND OF PISSED OFF.

SREE-EE-EE-EEE!
SHIT! UNICORNS ARE FUCKING RUDE!
TAKE COVER!

SERIOUSLY. A UNICORN? Y'ALL SCARED OF A UNICORN? I'LL HANDLE THIS.
EVOKAR PERCEPI--

FPAP

HNNG!
THUD

WHOAAA THERE, FELLA... HOLD ON NOW... HALT--ERR--STOP!

munch munch
NGAHHOWW!
SPLSH

SPLURCH
OH--
--MY--
--GODS, IT'S--
--I WON'T GO DOWNSTAIRS, DADDY, I PROMISE!

SOOO PRETTY...SOOO SMOOTH...MILKY BREATH...
MS. RED QUEEN? HELLOOO? CAN YOU HEAR ME?
WHERE YOU ARE... HORNED BABY... TASTE YOUR SMELL...

CUPCAKES AND LAVENDER... RIBBONS OF SILK... SHOW ME YOUR WINGS... FLY ME TO THE MOOOON...
OH ⸗KOFF⸗ MY. SHE'S SUCCUMBED. ⸗TT⸗ POOR THING.

AH WELL, LOST CAUSE--SHE'LL BE DEAD AND THERE'S SURELY NOTHING I CAN ⸗KOFF⸗ DO TO HELP THAT, EH, CHAUNCEY? MY DELICIOUSLY HANDSOME LITTLE ⸗KOFF⸗ MORSEL.
COME NOW, COME. LET US FIND A MORE...PRIVATE LOCALE TO SETTLE INTO.

HARK...HARK... TEA CUPS AND CARRIAGE PARTS...GIVE ME MY CHANGE...SHIT IN YOUR EYE...

OOH, THIS OUGHT TO DO, YES, THIS OUGHT TO DO JUST FINE. THE MOONLIGHT RADIATES FOR YOU, CHAUNCEY-BOY.
THERE. NICE AND ⸗KOFF⸗ COZY.

I LOVE YOU, ⸗KOFF⸗ CHAUNCEY.
MY PERFECT STEED. ALL I ⸗HAKK⸗ NEED.

RAHHHH!
...THE SLOG CHIMP!
I'M-I'M PISSING. RIGHT NOW. IT WON'T STOP.
HEY! WHAT'S UP? HOW'VE YOU BEE--

THWUMP

OH GODS OH GODS OH GODS OH GODS--

FFFUUGG THISSS...
SLOGGY, STOP! PUT HER DOWN, MAN! IT'S ME!

WHOA. *BETTY?*
YEAH! IT'S ME, REMEMBER?
HAHA. SHIIIT. I HAVEN'T SEEN YOU SINCE...
THAT NIGHT AFTER THE PEACH FESTIVAL, YEAH. THAT WAS INSANE--MAN, I WAS HUNG OVER FOR, LIKE, A FORTNIGHT.

HANNAH! YOU OKAY?
ARE YOU HURT? TALK TO US, BABE.
I'M... I'M FINE. JUST DON'T...DON'T TOUCH ME. LEAVE ME HERE...UNTIL IT DRIES.

THAT DUDE SENT YOU TO KILL ME? HAHA, WEIRD! THAT GUY IS NUTS, BETTY. LIKE, BETWEEN YOU ME...PRETTTTY SURE HE HAS "RELATIONS" WITH THE UNICORNS.
OH, HE *TOTALLY* DOES. HE'S GOT THIS SEVERED UNICORN HEAD WITH HIM AND...YEAHHH.

UNICORNS, MAN. I FUCKIN' HATE 'EM. NEVER HAVE I SEEN SUCH NASTY, MEAN ASSHOLES. THEY'RE THE WORST, BETTY.
HONESTLY, THAT'S THE ONLY REASON I STILL LIVE IN THIS DUMP–TO KILL THE LOT OF THOSE PRICKS. THEY NEST HERE. DISEASE-SPREADERS. *UNICHLAMYDIA*.
APPARENTLY I'M THE ONLY THING IMMUNE TO IT. I HATE KILLING--I'M A PACIFIST--BUT DAMN IT, I'LL DO MY PART IF IT MEANS RIDDING THE WORLD OF THOSE FUCKS.

UNICHLAMYDIA? I'VE NEVER HEARD OF THAT ONE.
FUCKING UNICORNS.
OH NO... *VIOLET*. SHE'S BEEN SICK ALONE WITH THAT OLD PERVERT'S PET HEAD.

OOF. YEAHHH, SHE GONNA DIE, MY DUDES. BUMMER.
YOUR BLOOD IS IMMUNE, SO I CAN ADD IT TO A HEALING SPELL. PLEASE, NOBLE SLOG CHIMP--WILL YOU HELP US HELP OUR SISTER?
YEAH, TOTALLY. UNLESS I SEE A UNICORN FIRST. THAT'S MY THING, SLAUGHTERING THOSE DICKS, LIKE I SAID.

SO. HOW'S SWAMP LIFE?
NAH, YEAH. IT'S GOOD. I MEAN, IT'S *OKAY.*
KINDA LONELY. BUT WHAT YOU GONNA DO?

I KNEW WE SHOULDN'T HAVE TAKEN THIS QUEST.
HAVE WE EVER HAD AN *EASY* ONE? LET'S JUST SAVE VIOLET AND GET BACK TO PALISADE.
NOT BEFORE I FIND THAT OLD CREEP AND INCINERATE HIS PRECIOUS CHAUNCEY.

HEY, CARL.
OH HEY, LINDA. WHAT'S UP?
THE RENT, MOTHER-FUCKER.
HAH. YOU'RE TELLIN' ME.

I TOLD YOU I KNEW HIM! PRETTY COOL GUY, RIGHT? HELL OF A SINGER TOO. HE HITS THESE HIGH NOTES AND ADDS A LITTLE BIT OF THAT, YOU KNOW, THROATY WARBLE, IT'S BEAUTIFUL.
YOU CAN UP-SELL THAT MONSTER ALL YOU WANT. I'M NEVER GOING TO SO MUCH AS LOOK AT THAT TH--
WUH-OH...

SHE'S GONE?
GOSSAMER MCHORSEPUMPER TOO. AND THAT FILTHY UNICORN HEAD OF HIS.
FUCKIN' UNICORNS, MAN.

VIOLET? VIOLET, YOU BITCH! I FUCKIN' LOVE YOU!
SHE...SHE MELTED!
COME BACK TO US, VIOLET! STAY OUT OF THE LIGHT!

SNFF SNFF
HOLD IT. A SMELL...

GRRRRRRRRR
AHHHH! OH FUCKITY HELL ASS!

THE HELL, SLOGGY?!
FOLLOW THAT CHIMP!

NICE... NICE GIRL... KOFF
SUMMER TIME KOFF DANCE...JUNIPER VELVET...
KOFF LOTION FUR...SILKY MANE...
...SWEET, SWEET KOFF FOREST BABES...
COME TO ME, MY DARLINGS KOFF
LET ME LOVE YOU SO...
VIOLET! WHAT ARE YOU DOING? GET OUT OF THERE!
UNICORNS ARE ASSHOLES! THEY'RE ASSSHOOOLES!

munch munch
munch munch
HURGURR BURGLE HMM FARFAR BEMBERR

RAHHHH!

HUFF!
THUD
SNWEEE!

CRUNCH
KRAK
BLRCH

GODS *DAMN.*
THIS IS THE MOST BRUTAL THING I'VE EVER SEEN IN MY LIFE.
YET... REMARKABLY BEAUTIFUL.

≈HNNF!≈
SHUNK

UGH, THEY'RE SURPRISINGLY EASY TO CUT THROUGH.
SHICK

BZZZZT
LIKE BUTTER, RIGHT? BARF!

I'M TRYING TO MAKE IT QUICK, YOU FOOL! LET ME END YOU!
WEHHH

YOU GAVE US QUITE THE SCARE THERE, VI. HOW YOU FEELING?
YOUR SPELL'S KICKING IN. BUT I DON'T REMEMBER ANYTHING.
MAYBE IT'S FOR THE BEST. YOU GOT REAL WEIRD THERE. WE'LL REMIND YOU NEXT TIME YOU WON'T PAY FOR DRINKS.

VIOLET, YOU'RE AWAKE! OH, THANK SLOG. YOU MISSED SOME SERIOUS SHIT. DID YOU KNOW THAT UNICORNS ARE ACTUALLY THE WORST?

THANKS FOR THE SAVE. SO THE BIG BEDTIME STORY IS REAL, HUH? WHERE'S GOSSAMER--LET'S AT LEAST GET PAID FOR ALL THIS.
YEAHHH, ABOUT THAT...

"...WE FOUND HIM AND CHAUNCEY A FEW MILES AWAY. RIGOR MORTIS ALREADY SET IN. STILL CLUTCHING THAT AWFUL UNICORN HEAD."
"HE DIED AS HE LIVED--BEING A FRIGGING PERVERT WHO DOESN'T PAY UP."

WELP. ALL'S WELL THAT ENDS WELL? TIME TO PARTY, I GUESS.
OH HELL YEAH. NOTHING TIGHTENS ME UP LIKE A BIG OL' 'CORN KILLIN'.

HONESTLY, SWAMP-LIVIN' AIN'T THAT BAD. I GOT A GOOD THING GOING. OH, AND I'M GETTING MY REAL ESTATE LICENSE PRETTY SOON. THINK I MIGHT START FLIPPING SOME BOGS.
I HEAR IT CAN BE PHOO VERY HIKK LUCRATIVE, YES.
UGH, I CAN STILL SMELL THEM. I'LL NEVER EAT A CUPCAKE AGAIN. ALSO, WHY IS THERE TREE SAP IN MY ASS?
KEEP DIGGING! HORNWOOD'S FORTUNE HAS TO BE HERE SOMEWHERE. THAT BASTARD WAS CRAZY ENOUGH TO ACTUALLY BURY IT IN THIS HELL-HOLE.
RNNF!
I'LL DIG A HOLE TO THE OTHER SIDE OF THIS WORLD IF IT GETS ME AWAY FROM THE SLOG CHIMP.

CHAPTER SIXTEEN

The Kingdom of Blorevion. One year ago.

P-PLEASE... THIS IS WILDLY UNNECESSARY. WHATEVER YOU WANT, IT'S YOURS!
I WANT AN AUDIENCE. WITH YOUR KING.
W-WE ARE A P-PEACEFUL KINGDOM. PACIFISTS. THE KING WILL SEE ANYONE!

LOOK-- COMPANY. AT ATTENTION! ACT BUSY!
HOH THERE, FRIEND! HOW LOVELY TO RECEIVE A VISIT FROM ONE OF MY MANY HAPPY DENIZENS OF BLOREVION.

WHAT BRINGS YOU TO MY CHAMBER, MY GOOD--HMM... I'M SORRY, I CANNOT QUITE RECOGNIZE YOU.
WHY NOT REMOVE YOUR OUTERWEARS AND ENJOY A DRINK WITH THE KING?

I'M NOT HERE TO DRINK UNTIL I'VE EMPTIED YOU OF BLOOD, YOUR HIGHNESS.
SHIK

OH SHHHII--
SHICK

HEY WAIT PLEASE STOP NO DON'T WHY--
STAB

WHAT IN THE GODS' BLUE HELL ARE YOU DOING? WE ARE A PEACEFUL KINGDOM!
WE HAVE NOT THE MEANS TO FIGHT, NOR WOULD WE WANT TO!

EXACTLY.
THAT IS WHY YOU HAVE FALLEN...

SHRAK

..AND WHY I WILL SAVE MY KINGDOM.

The rainforest of J'aalhuul. Present day.
NNNGGRRAARRGGH!
WE CAN TAKE THIS THING DOWN! JUST KEEP AT IT!
"KEEP AT IT?" I CAN BARELY KEEP MY LUNCH DOWN.
MAYBE SOMEONE SHOULDN'T HAVE DRANK TILL SUNUP KNOWING WE'D BE FIGHTING THE FREAKING ***GOLGARAKK*** THE NEXT DAY.
I...I CANT =HUFF= DO IT, BRAGA. IT'S =HUFF= TRUE--I'M THE WORST RAT QUEEN.
MADDIE, STOP. YOU ***WILL*** GET FIRED FOR THAT... BUT NEVER FOR TRYING.
TAKE MY HAND.

ACK!
SWOOSH
GET UP THERE AND DO SOMETHING. TAKE OUT THAT FRUSTRATION.
ATTA GIRL, MADDIE ≶HNG≶ YOU'RE DOING ≶URFF≶ GREAT.
GODS, YOU'RE A LI'L FOUNTAIN OF PUKE TODAY.

WWOOAHWOAH!

YOU WERE HAVING FUN LAST NIGHT TOO. WHAT'S WITH YOU LATELY?
HM? ME? NOTHING.
YOU DONE BARFING? WANNA JOIN US?

≶HNG!≶ AHH, C'MON!
DEE, I THINK IT'S TIME...

MADDIE'S RIGHT--WE CAN'T GET OUT OF THIS ONE.
WE ARE BLOWING IT. BIG TIME.
JUST GIVE US AN EASY WIN FOR ONCE. PLEASE? YOU'RE A GOD.

THUD
OOF!
OKAY, I'M DONE. GETTING A BIT TIRED OF BEING ASKED TO SNAP MY FINGERS AND FIX ALL OUR SHIT, TO BE HONEST.
EVOKAR BLASTISUMAX.
FSSST
FOR FUCK'S SAKE.
DEE, WAIT-- IT'S NOT LIKE THAT.
H'OKAY, I GUESS THAT'S THAT THEN. QUEST FAILED. AGAIN.
I NEED HAIR...OF THE DOG. BE A DOLL AND CARRY ME TO MAESTRO'S.

YOU'RE NO KING. THE RESISTANCE WILL LIVE ON!
EVERYONE HATES YOU... YOU KNOW THAT? EVEN THE ONES THAT CLAIM LOYALTY.
TO THEM YOU'RE NOTHING BUT...

HM. GO ON. SAY IT.

"...A REAL ASSHOLE."

Present Day.
Formerly the Kingdom of Blorevion.

THE KING! OUR KING HAS RETURNED!
KNEEL FOR HIS HIGHNESS, YOU CUNTS!

RISE.
YOU HAVE BEEN LOYAL IN THE WAKE OF BLOREVION'S *REVOLT.*
WE HAVE SUCCEEDED. I KILLED THE LAST OF THE TRAITORS.

THOUGH IT CAME AT A GREAT COST-- OUR HOME.

WHAT WE DO NO HOME THEN?
WHERE WE US SLEEP?

I WILL LEAD YOU TO A NEW KINGDOM, OF COURSE! WE WILL MAKE OUR OWN HOME. ONE THAT ISN'T UNGRATEFUL. THAT WON'T RESIST.
ONE WORTHY OF BEING CONQUERED BY A NEW KING.

FULL SPEED AHEAD...

"...I KNOW JUST THE PLACE."

BETTYYY, HEYYY. YOU'RE...HEEERE, YEAHHH.
PLEASE, BE WELCOMED INTO MY HOME.
HANNAH, STOP BEING WEIRD ABOUT IT!

HEY, Y'ALL, I WAS THINKIN' ABOUT THE RAT QUEENS AND--HEAR ME OUT HERE-- NETWORKING.
UHH. WHY... WHY ARE Y'ALL SO LONG IN THE FACE? WAIT-- DID SOMEONE DIE?

SHOULD I BE HERE? I FEEL LIKE I'M TOO NEW TO BE HERE.
BETTY. LOOK AROUND THIS ROOM. WHAT YOU SEE ARE SOME PEOPLE WHO JUST LOVE YOU LIKE CRAZY.
WE'RE JUST GOING TO SAY SOME THINGS, THEN YOU'RE GOING TO SAY SOME THINGS, AND--

HOLD UP. NO. NNNOOOO.
IS THIS... HAH...OH GODS... IS THIS AN INTERVENTION?

BETTY, YOU HAVE A DRINKING PROBLEM. BUT YOU'RE NOT ALONE IN THIS AND WE JUST WANT--

YOU'RE BEING AN INSANELY HUGE ASSHOLE AND YOU STINK LIKE THE UNDERCARRIAGE OF A GNARGNOTH.

IT'S TRUE. YOU USED TO SMELL FRESH. OF LAVENDER!

WOULD YOU TWO CALM IT? WE'RE TRYING TO *HELP* HER, NOT SHAME HER INTO SOBRIETY.
SINCE WHEN ARE YOU THE CALM ONE?
SINCE SHE DROPPED US TO TEACH MADDIE ALL HER ORC TRICKS.

BUT-BUT... YOU *ASKED* ME TO JOIN YOU...
THERE THERE, IT'S OKAY. PART OF BECOMING A RAT QUEEN IS ENDURING THOUSANDS OF HOURS OF TORMENT AND RIDICULE.
DROPPED YOU? IN CASE YOU HAVEN'T NOTICED, WE *SUCK* LATELY.
IF ANYONE'S DROPPED US, IT'S DEE--WE FOUGHT A GIANT FREAKING SPIDER AND SHE JUST BAILED ON US!

I'M NOT YOUR LITTLE *GOD TOY!* YOU TREAT ME LIKE I'M NOT EVEN THE SAME PERSON ANYMORE!

OH PUHH-LEASE CRY ME A RIVER-- I *LITERALLY* LOST A PIECE OF MYSELF!

OKAY, FINE! I'LL QUIT DRINKING! I'LL QUIT PARTYING!
AND IF WE KEEP BEING TOTAL FUCKING BITCHES TO EACH OTHER...

...I'LL QUIT US TOO. JUST LIKE VIOLET.

WE CAN DO THIS, BETTS.
YEAH. TOGETHER.
WE'RE HERE FOR YOU.

I DON'T NEED TO GET TRASHED. WHAT I NEED IS ALL OF *YOU*.
BUT WE'RE *DYING*. I CAN FEEL IT.

A LOT HAS HAPPENED IN THE LAST YEAR. BUT WE'LL GET OURSELVES BACK.
'KAY. I'M GONNA GO DO...NOT DRINKING?
SORRY, BETTY.

THIS IS A FAMILY, MADDIE.
THE BAD STUFF HURTS. DEEP. BE PREPARED FOR THAT.

One week later. Palisade Job Fair.
I CAN'T BELIEVE WE'RE DOING THIS. I'D GIVE MY OTHER ARM TO GET PAID FOR A QUEST, LIKE A NORMAL, SELF-RESPECTING PERSON.
I HATE BEING BROKE. NOW WE HAVE TO WORK? PROVIDING GOODS AND OR SERVICES?
HOW ABOUT A CAREER IN DAIRY? PALISADE IS THE LAND OF MILK AND HONEY. IT'S BUTTER THAN UNEMPLOYMENT--JOIN ME AND CHURN YOUR KEEP!
OH GODS, I NEED A SHOWER.
EUGH, I NEED AN ALE.
SO, YEAH...I DIDN'T KNOW IF I SHOULD ASK...BUT HOW'S THAT...GOING? YOU HAVEN'T...
NOOO, HANNAHHH. I HAVEN'T. DON'T WORRY. BUT HONESTLY? IT'S REALLY, REALLY HARD.
IT'S, LIKE, EVERYTHING I DO, MY REACTION IS TO DRINK. GOOD NEWS? THROW ONE BACK. BAD NEWS? TAKE A SWIG.
IT'S BEEN A WEEK AND I'M CRAWLING OUT MY SKIN, HANNAH.

I HAD AN IDEA--A SPELL THAT MIGHT HELP YOU. KIND OF A SUPPORT SYSTEM. BUT IT'S NOT...THERE YET.
EVER SINCE I LOST MY ARM THINGS HAVE JUST FELT OFF. I CAN'T CAST LIKE BEFORE. MY BRAIN ACTIVELY HATES THE REST OF ME.
IT'S FUCKING TORTURE.
YEAH. IT WAS MY DIDDLIN' HAND TOO.
REMEMBER WHEN ALL THIS WAS FUN?

AY! CHICKIE! PSST! C'MERE!
WANNA MAKE SOME *REAL* MONEY?

WHO WANTS A JOB WHEN YOU CAN MAKE A FORTUNE IN A MINUTE, EH?
ALLS Y'GOTTA DO IS PICK THE DEATH CARD.

'ROUND AN' 'ROUND IT GOES, WHERE IT STOPS, NOBODY--
IT'S UNDERNEATH THE BOX. YOU'RE JUST SHUFFLING THE LIFE, WEALTH, AND GLUTTON CARDS.

BUT HOW--HOW DID YOU KNOW...
I'LL TAKE THAT. *HMM*, TWO-HUNDRED? THAT'S ALL? MAYBE *YOU* OUGHT TO GET OUT THERE AND FIND A NEW JOB.

NO...NOT FAIR...YOU *SWINDLED* ME!
YOU CHEATED!

YOU AIN'T NO REG'LAR GIRL-O...
...SOMETHIN' VERY OFF ABOUT YOU...
SIGH

YOU JOINED AT A WEIRD TIME, MADDIE. NORMALLY WE MAKE LOADS OF--OH, WHO AM I KIDDING, WE NEVER MADE MONEY.
I'M JUST SAYING IT'S IMPORTANT TO KEEP YOURSELF FULFILLED. YOUR MIND... ORGANIZED.

WE BRING OURSELVES TO THIS GROUP. LIKE, OUR FEELINGS. IF ONE OF US SUFFERS, EVENTUALLY WE ALL DO.
CUTTING YOURSELF OFF--PUTTING UP WALLS--IT'S A SLOW POISON. YOU KNOW?

BRAGA, WHY ARE YOU HELPING ME SO MUCH? I'M NOT BIG AND STRONG. I'M NOT GOOD WITH A SWORD--WITH ANYTHING.
HECK, I'M TINY BUT NOT EVEN *FAST*.
SPLURCH

I DON'T BELIEVE I CAN BE BOTH, LIKE YOU. MASSIVE AND POWERFUL AND SMART AND NICE.
I'M SUPPOSED TO BE ME AND MAYBE THAT'S ALL I'LL BE--JUST QUIET AND SLOW AND... ADEQUATE.

YOU KNOW THE SHIT I'VE HAD TO GO THROUGH? HOW HARD IT IS TO MAINTAIN THAT BALANCE? IT'S WORK, MADDIE.
I'M TRYING TO *TEACH* YOU. SOMETHING I NEVER GOT. GO FIND A DESK JOB IF THIS IS SO HARD FOR YOU.

UHH, HANNAH? I'VE BEEN GETTIN' THE SHAKES, BUT DO YOU FEEL THAT?
I'VE SAT ON MY FAIR SHARE OF SPIN-CYCLES, BUT YEAH--DEFINITELY AN EARTHQUAKE.
RRRRRRRRRRRRRUUWUU

UUUUMMMMMMMMMMMM
SOMETHING UNDER THE GROUND!
NUH-UH! IT'S SOMETHING FROM THE SKY!

MMMMMBBBBBBBB
TERRORISTS!
EVERYBODY RUN!
MADDIE? MADDIE, WHERE'D YOU GO?

H-H-HELP...
LLLLLLLLLEEEEEEE

KABOOM
OH HOLY FUCK-HORNS! LET'S GET THE GALS. THIS IS NO EARTHQUAKE...

...IT'S A GODSDAMN ATTACK!
ALL RIGHT, LI'L STRAIGHT-EDGE. WE GOTTA DANCE.
DO WE, LIKE...OWE ANY MONEY? THERE'S SO MUCH I BLACKED OUT ON.
HANNAH! BETTY! YOU GOOD?
THWAK
NOPE! NOT FUCKING GOOD AT ALL! YOU KNOW ANYTHING ABOUT THIS?
NOPE TOO! BUT I AM GETTING A WEIRD...DEJA VU?
HOLD ON, MADDIE, I GOT YOU!
I FEEL AT EASE AGAINST YOUR BOSOM.
REMEMBER-- THINK CLEAR. STRIKE ONCE. FEEL THE GROUND. MOVE WITH PURPOSE.
LADIES.
DEE. STILL DOING SHIT-ALL TO FIX THIS?
HANNAH, CHILL!
FORM A PHALANX! WE CAN ALTERNATE STRIKES!
THERE'S ONLY FIVE OF US! WHO ARE THEY? *WHAT IS HAPPENING?!*

THAT THEM.
MUSH 'EM.
YEP, THEM THERE.

LOOK OUT, BABE!
HGULK!
THUD

YES! THAT'S IT, MADDIE! BATTLE IS A SONG...
...PLAY IT WITH GRACE, PRECISION, AND INTENT.
SWISH

SHE'S ONE OF THEM! HOLD HER!
HNNNG
NOOO, DEE--YOU CAN'T.

WELL THIS IS JUST FUCKIN' PEACHY...
PARRPA
PRAPP
ALL KNEEL FOR THE KING OF BLOREVION!
BLOREVION? NEVER HEARD OF IT.
SOUNDS LIKE A BUNCH OF ASSHOLES TO ME.
AHH, PALISADE. YOU HAVEN'T CHANGED ONE BIT. BUT YOU WILL.
ALL THE PRIVILEGES AND SPOILS YOU'VE INDULGED IN? YYYEAH, BUH-BYE.
TAKE A GOOOOD LAST LOOK AROUND YOU. YOU'RE IN MY KINGDOM NOW.
AND AS FOR YOU...THE INCORRIGIBLE, INFAMOUS RAT QUEENS?
I'M GOING TO ENJOY HEARING YOUR FINAL BREATHS AS YOU UTTER THE WORDS...

...ALL HAIL KING GARY!
WHAT AN ASSHOLE.

CHAPTER SEVENTEEN

HELLOOOO, RAT QUEENS!
YOU LOOK...DIFFERENT. WHERE'S GINGER SNATCH? AND WHO'S THE DWEEB?
KING GARY-- I'M ROYALTY, VIZARI. I OWN A CASTLE. AND HUGE BOATS. I'M VERY SUCCESSFUL NOW, YOU SEE.
GARY, YOU ASSHOLE, LET US OUT OR I'LL--
MOST WOULD PROBABLY SAY "SEXY" EVEN.

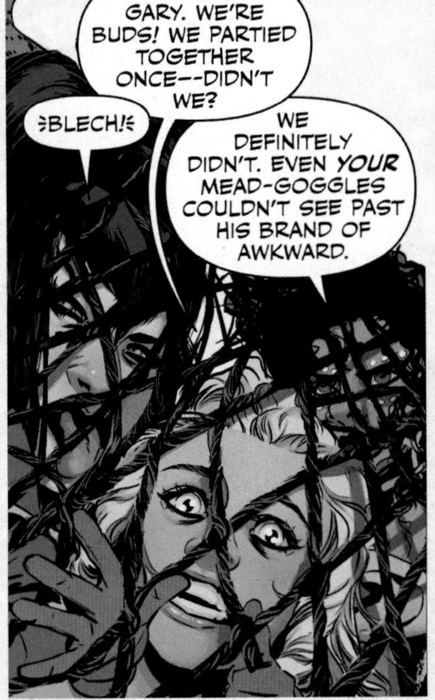
C'MON, GARY. WE'RE BUDS! WE PARTIED TOGETHER ONCE--DIDN'T WE?
BLECH!
WE DEFINITELY DIDN'T. EVEN YOUR MEAD-GOGGLES COULDN'T SEE PAST HIS BRAND OF AWKWARD.

AND WHO ARE YOU? HMM?
NOT IMPORTANT. YOU KNOW, YOU SHOULD ALIGN YOURSELF WITH SOME BETTER COMPANY.
EVERYONE KNOWS THE RAT QUEENS ARE JERKS. REAL BIG ONES.

TAKE A GOOOOD, LONG LOOK AT ME NOW, BRAT QUEEFS. DIDN'T SEE THIS COMING, EH?
"THAT GARY'S A REAL ASSHOLE. WHAT A LOSER," THEY SAID. "GARY SMELLS LIKE PISSY FORESKIN AND MUSHROOM SOUP," THEY TOLD ME.
SURPRISE! YOU ARE THE ASSHOLES. YOU AND EVERYONE ELSE IN PALISADE.

IS HE... IS HE SERIOUSLY *THE VILLAIN*?
FINE, WE GET IT, GARY. YOU'RE COOL AND SUCCESSFUL NOW. WE'RE IMPRESSED. OH WOW.
SO NOW WHAT? YOU CAN'T JUST CONQUER AN ENTIRE CITY LIKE PALISADE.

YES I CAN. I CAN DO WHATEVER I WANT. AND WHAT I WANT IS TO DO THAT, AND I'M GOING TO-- I *HAVE* DONE IT.

I CAN DO WHAT I WANT BECAUSE IT'S WHAT I WANT TO DO, AND NO ONE CAN TELL ME I CAN'T ANYMORE!

OTHER GARY AND OTHER OTHER GARY!
GET THE RAT QUEENS OUT OF MY SIGHT.
YEH, BOSS.
IT ME.

GARY, YOU ASSHOLE, YOU'VE LOST YOUR DAMNED MIND!
PUT THEM WITH THE OTHERS UNTIL I CAN FIGURE OUT WHAT ABSURDLY HORRIBLE THING TO DO WITH THEM...

"...THEY NEED TO LEARN THEY ARE NOTHING SPECIAL."
Y'ALL KEEP QUIET NOW. POSITIVELY NO HOOTERIN' IN HERE.
HEY. DICKHEAD. I NEED A BATHROOM.
CONGRATS. YOUR GASTROINTESTINAL SYSTEM WORKS.
GASP YOU SALTY BITCH.
IT'S A ONE, NOT A TWO. FUCKFACE.

THEY EXPECT US TO JUST USE THE FLOOR. JUST ANOTHER TUESDAY FOR US THOUGH, HAHA, RIGHT?
DEE, I'M REFUSING TO TALK TO YOU UNTIL YOU DO THE RIGHT THING--FOR EVERYONE ELSE BUT YOU--AND SNAP YOUR FINGERS OR WHATEVER AND GET US OUT OF HERE.

HANNAH, PLEASE. THAT'S NOT FAIR. THIS ISN'T EASY FOR ME.
IT'S ABOUT ABSOLUTE MORALI--

HEY, BETTS. SO. WHATCHA THINKIN' 'BOUT?
NGUH HANNAH?

I THINK... I THINK I'M *DYING*.

I CAN'T BELIEVE THIS.
YOU DON'T GET IT, MADDIE.
YEAH. BUT LOOK ON THE BRIGHT SIDE. WE'RE ALL HERE TOGETHER, HAH.

I'M THE *TOUGH* ONE. THE MUSCLE. I'M SUPPOSED TO BREAK THROUGH THINGS AND SMASH THINGS.
I DON'T GET CAPTURED.

SO...I DON'T "GET IT" BECAUSE I'M NOT BIG AND STRONG?
LIKE, LOSING IS SOMETHING THAT SHOULD JUST COME NATURALLY TO SOMEONE LIKE ME?

AND YOU WONDER WHY I NEVER TRY NEW THINGS, OR--GODS FORBID--HAVE THE CONFIDENCE TO STAND UP FOR MYSELF.
IT'S JUST ASSUMED THAT I'M USELESS, SO MY BRAIN DOUBLES-DOWN ON BEING TERRIFIED OF *LITERALLY EFFING EVERYTHING!*

IF I'M IGNORED ONE MORE TIME, I SWEAR TO GODS I'M GOING TO...I'M GOING TO...
HRRRRUH!

I CAN'T BELIEVE THIS...SORRY, MADDIE. WHAT WERE YOU SAYING?

N-NOTHING.

YOU'RE NOT DYING, MY LITTLE ROSEBUD--YOU'VE GOT THE BOOZE ***WITHDRAWALS***.
WHAT'S IT BEEN, LIKE, FIVE MINUTES? HAH.

THIS IS WORSE THAN THE HANGOVERS. I'M DESPERATE, HANNAH!
GET ME A TOILET AND TWO TURNIPS--NO, THREE BEETS!--...I'LL DO THE REST...SWEET, SWEET PRISON WINE.

OKAY, BETTY. =SIGH= I DON'T SEE ANY OTHER OPTION. YOU NEED SOME... ***EXTERNAL SUPPORT.***
I'M RUSTY. LORD HELP US ALL IF THIS DOESN'T WORK.

EVOKAR SUBLIMINOSA!
BZZZZT
UHHH, HANNAH? WHAT ARE YOU DOING TO ME?

I CAN FEEL MY CELLS JIGGLING!

WHAT THE...
SQUELCH
BLOODY FUCKIN' HELL!

OH MY GODS, IT WORKED?
THAT CAME OUT OF ME? AM I A... *MOM*?

NOT SO FAST...
...I AM *YOU*--WELL, THE PART THAT AIN'T A SHIT-FACED, DRUNKEN LOUT.
NAME'S *TERWILLIGER*. I'M YER SPIRITUAL SPONSOR. YER CONSCIENCE, AS IT WERE.
AND I'M GONNA WHIP YER TINY ASS INTO *SOBRIETY*.

BRILLIANT IDEA. GOOD JOB, HANNAH.
IGNORING. BUT YES, I KNOW.

I LIKE YOUR STYLE, TERWILLIGER!

OR-- WAIT-- ***MY STYLE?*** DAMN, I'M COOL. VERY "WITH IT."

THIS IS ALL CUTE AND I SUPPORT YOUR EFFORTS OF SOBRIETY, BETTY...

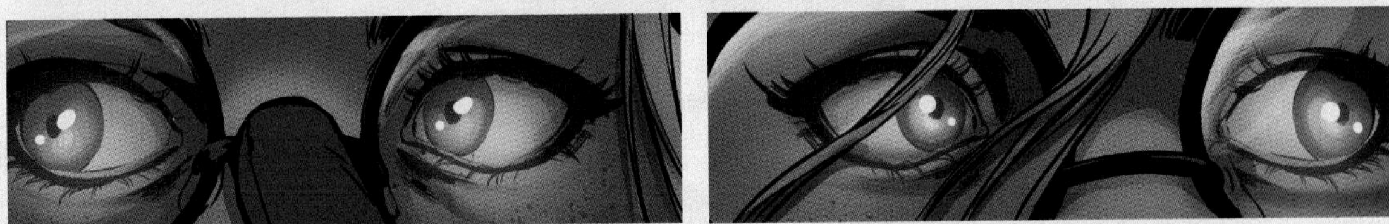

...BUT WE REALLY NEED TO FOCUS ON HOW WE *GET OUT OF HERE*.

HEY. REAL TALK. DOES THIS STUFF...I DUNNO, *DEPRESS* YOU?
WHADDAYA MEAN? YOU OKAY, MAN? FEELING DOWN?
I MEAN... YEAH. A LITTLE.
GARY'S GREAT, DON'T GET ME WRONG. AND I DO LOVE PILLAGING. LIKE, A LOT.
IT IS FUN. HE'S GIVEN US SO MUCH. SELFLESS, OUR KING.
RIGHT, BUT, LIKE, DO YOU EVER WANT TO DO SOMETHING ELSE? WITH *LIFE*, I MEAN.

YOU KNOW...I DO. THERE'S SOMETHING THAT I'VE WANTED FOREVER. I'VE NEVER TOLD ANYONE.
YOU TOO? I'LL TELL IF YOU TELL.
OHMYGODS. OKAY.

I WANT TO DANCE.
I WANT TO DANCE.
OHMYGODS.
LET'S.

HEY. YER THINKIN' ABOUT THE TAVERN AGAIN. KNOCK THAT SHIT OFF.
SORRY, TERWILLIGER.
HANNAH, PLEASE...

THAT'S IT. I CAN'T TAKE IT ANYMORE. I'M LOSING MY DAMNED MIND.
HHRRNNG!

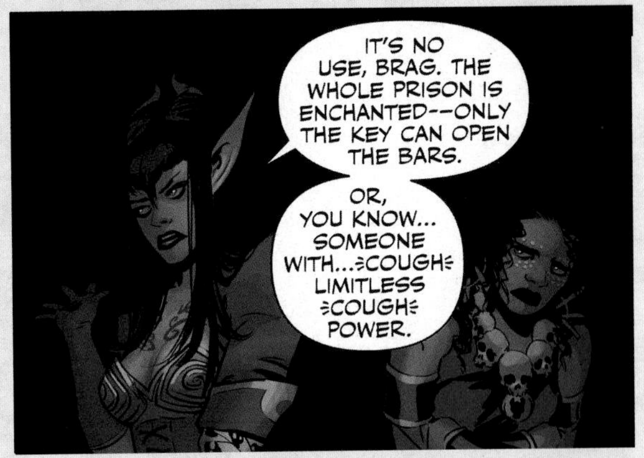
IT'S NO USE, BRAG. THE WHOLE PRISON IS ENCHANTED--ONLY THE KEY CAN OPEN THE BARS.
OR, YOU KNOW... SOMEONE WITH... COUGH LIMITLESS COUGH POWER.

I HAVE THE KEY. I TOOK IT.
BRILLIANT! A LADY OF RESULTS.
MADDIE?!

OH, MADDIE--YOU DID IT? I DIDN'T THINK YOU COULD!
YEAH. I DID. AND... THANKS?
I'VE TAUGHT YOU SO WELL.

OH-HOHOHO NO YA DON'T!
YA CAN SIP MY ASS FER ALL THE GOOD IT'LL DO YA!
JUST ONE SIP! PLEASE! TO TAKE THE EDGE OFF!

NICE, THAT WAS JUST A LITTLE SOMETHING I WROTE. IT'S NOTHING REALLY. FROM THE HEART THOUGH, FOR SURE. SUPER GOOD, RIGHT?
YES, MY LORD. TRULY...GOOD. INDEED.
YEAH, SOULFUL. GREAT VIBES HERE TONIGHT. REALLY FEELING CONNECTED, Y'KNOW? *MMM.*
OKAY, COOL, HERE'S ANOTHER ONE. I WROTE IT. KIND OF A LOVE THING...

SO... WHAT'S THE PLAN NOW? WE LEAVE PALISADE, NEVER TO RETURN EVER AGAIN?
I'M ACTUALLY OKAY WITH THAT. DESPITE IT BEING, YOU KNOW, COMPLETELY UNHEROIC.
OOH! NEW IDENTITIES! I WANNA BE A RIVERBOAT PIANIST!
NO. WE'RE ALL GOING BACK TO PALISADE...
...BUT WE CAN'T DO IT ALONE.

"WE NEED HELP."

nok
nok
"WE NEED *HER*."

HEY. YOU OKAY?
YEAH. I'M JUST...IT'S BEEN SO LONG. I'M SIMULTANEOUSLY WANTING THIS AND DREADING IT.

QUIT SHAKIN'. YER MAKIN' ME NAUSEOUS.
I CAN'T DO IT, TERWILLIGER. ALL I WANT TO DO IS HAVE FUN.
I DON'T KNOW HOW TO HAVE FUN ANY OTHER WAY THAN PARTYING, AND I'M FEELING WAY TOO MUCH RIGHT NOW.

YA HAVEN'T BEEN FEELIN' TOO MUCH FOR A WHILE NOW. AN' THAT'S THE PROBLEM. BOOZIN' MEANT YA DIN'T HAVE TA FEEL ANYTHIN'.
YOU'RE JUST A BIG, FAT SCAREDY-CAT.

SOMEONE'S ANSWERING...
OHMYGODS BREATHEHANNAH.

KNOCK AGAIN AND PULL BACK A STUMP! RETURN AND STAY IN PIECES!

OH.
IT'S YOU. WHAT ARE YOU DOING HERE?

WE NEED HELP, DAVE.
PALISADE. I KNOW. WE'VE HEARD. YOU CAN SEE WHY I'M A LITTLE ON EDGE WITH VISITORS.

WHICH IS EXACTLY WHY I NEED TO ASK YOU ALL TO LEAVE RIGHT N--

RAHHHH!
DALEN, NO!

ACK! GET THIS MONSTER KID OFF OF ME!

DALEN, NO. REMEMBER WHAT WE'VE BEEN PRACTICING. KINDNESS. BE KIND.
TREAT HOW YOU WANT TO BE TREATED. RIGHT?
GRRF

SORRY. DALEN'S DOING REALLY GREAT, BUT SOMETIMES HAS A LAPSE WHEN NEW THINGS HAPPEN.
KID'S GOT GUMPTION. I LIKE.
S-SORRY.

DAVE? WHAT'S GOING ON?
VI, IT'S...

OH MY GODS.

HANNAH, IT'S GOOD TO--
FUCK YOU, VIOLET.
YOU TOOK THE HEART OUT OF US. AND NOW? NOW WE TOTALLY SUCK.
HANNAH, STOP. SHE--
THAT FUCKING ASSHOLE GARY--HE'S ACTUALLY DONE IT, HE'S TAKEN OUR HOME, AND MAYBE WE DESERVE IT.
BUT WE'RE NOTHING WITHOU YOU, AND WE JUST. CAN'T. DO IT.
PLEASE. I KNOW YOU SAID YOU WER DONE, BUT...WE REALLY, REALL NEED YOU ON THIS ONE.
NO. I'M SORRY, BUT NO.
I CAN'T GO WITH YOU...
...WITH GOOD REASON.

HE'S REALLY GOOD WITH HIM.

HONESTLY, I CAN'T BELIEVE IT. HE IS JUST SO AMAZING. I'M HAPPY.
LIKE, REALLY HAPPY.

ALL I HAVE IS TEA, SORRY. BABY-ON-BOARD MEANS NO MORE WINE.
TEA'S JUST FINE, THANKS. YES. TEA. DELICIOUS FUCKIN' *TEA*, BETTY. LOOK.

IT'S GOOD TO SEE BETTY MORE... CHILL. THINGS GOT A BIT OUT OF HAND AT MY GOING AWAY PARTY.
MAESTRO LITERALLY PULLED HALF HIS BEARD OUT. LIFE-BANNED.

HERE YOU GO, MADDIE. STILL ENJOY BEING A RAT QUEEN?
I LOVE YOU. UHH-- I MEAN--I WISH I WAS MORE LIKE YOU.
IT'S FINE. I'M FINE. OHGODS.

THIS IS A LOVELY TEA PARTY, AND WE'RE ALL REALLY HAPPY FOR YOUR PEDIGREED UTERUS, BUT IF YOU CAN'T HELP US, WE HAVE TO GO.
KING ASSLORD IS OBVIOUSLY PETTY ENOUGH TO LOOK FOR US. WE CAN'T STAY HERE. YOU'RE WELCOME.

CONGRATS, VI. IT'S BEEN A SLICE.
HANNAH, STOP! WHY ARE YOU BEING LIKE THIS?
JUST... GIVE HER A LITTLE BIT. SHE'LL CALM DOWN. I THINK.

IF I'M BEING HONEST, I WASN'T EXPECTING THIS FROM YOU. MAYBE IT WAS DELUSIONAL WHEN I THOUGHT LEAVING WOULDN'T AFFECT THE RAT QUEENS...
...BUT IT MAKES ME SAD TO SEE MY SISTERS LIKE THIS.

AW, LOOK. SHE'S SNOOZING. I'M SO CUTE.
IT'S NOT LIKE WE WANT THINGS THIS WAY, VI. WE'RE JUST AS SAD ABOUT IT.
YEAH, AND THEN WE GET ANGRY FOR BEING SAD AND THEN IT'S...BYE BYE, CONTROL--HELLO, SELF-DESTRUCTIVE SPIRAL.
WE'RE OUR OWN WORST ENEMIES.

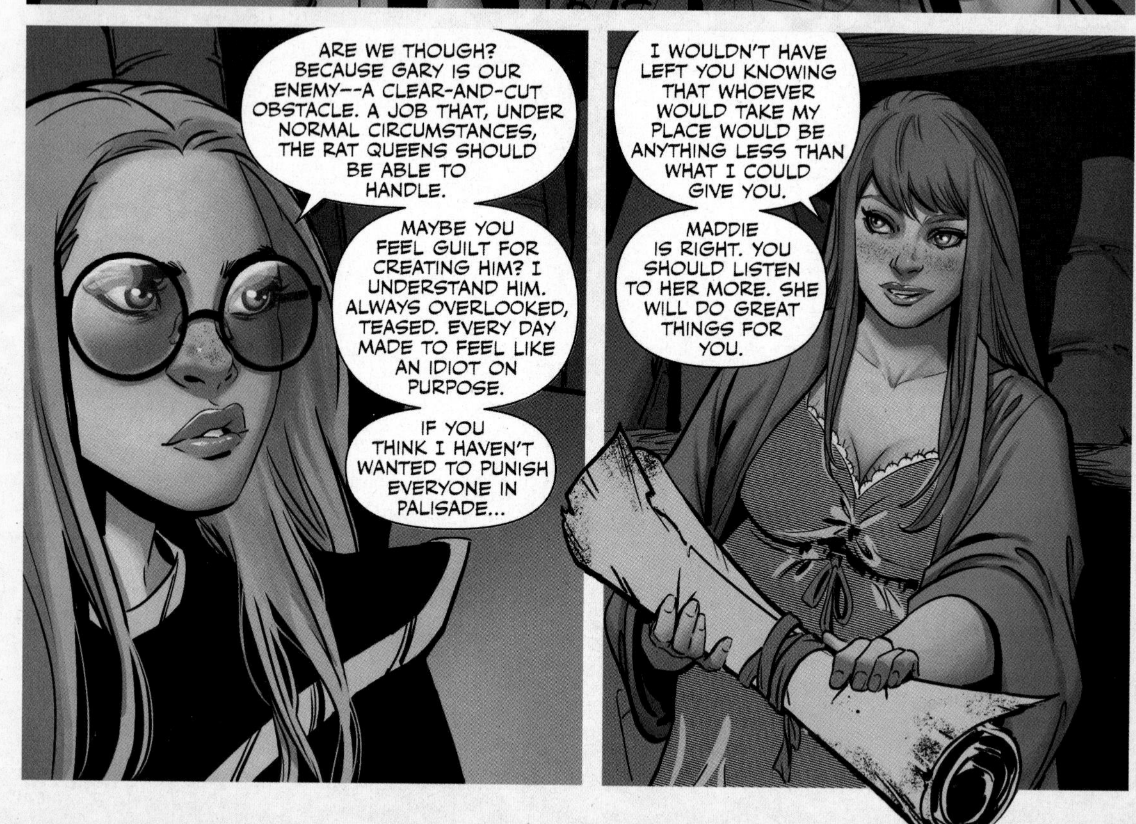
ARE WE THOUGH? BECAUSE GARY IS OUR ENEMY--A CLEAR-AND-CUT OBSTACLE. A JOB THAT, UNDER NORMAL CIRCUMSTANCES, THE RAT QUEENS SHOULD BE ABLE TO HANDLE.
MAYBE YOU FEEL GUILT FOR CREATING HIM? I UNDERSTAND HIM. ALWAYS OVERLOOKED, TEASED. EVERY DAY MADE TO FEEL LIKE AN IDIOT ON PURPOSE.
IF YOU THINK I HAVEN'T WANTED TO PUNISH EVERYONE IN PALISADE...
I WOULDN'T HAVE LEFT YOU KNOWING THAT WHOEVER WOULD TAKE MY PLACE WOULD BE ANYTHING LESS THAN WHAT I COULD GIVE YOU.
MADDIE IS RIGHT. YOU SHOULD LISTEN TO HER MORE. SHE WILL DO GREAT THINGS FOR YOU.

WE ARE SO HAPPY FOR YOU AND DAVE, VIOLET. IT WAS GOOD TO SEE YOU.
DON'T WORRY ABOUT HANNAH...SHE JUST HAS TO UNPACK SOME STUFF. YOU KNOW SHE LOVES YOU.
I KNOW.

WAIT! I'VE GOT ONE MORE THING. I SAID I COULDN'T GO *WITH* YOU...BUT I DIDN'T SAY I WOULDN'T *HELP.*
YOU SHOULD KNOW ME BETTER THAN THAT, C'MON NOW.

A... A MAP? I DON'T GET IT.
BETTER YET--A *WEAPON.*

AFTER I LEFT, I HID IT, OUT OF ANYONE ELSE'S GRASP, FOR A MOMENT EXACTLY LIKE THIS--WHEN EVERYTHING SEEMS IMPOSSIBLE.
THE MOST *POWERFUL* WEAPON YOU COULD IMAGINE. IT WILL DEFEAT GARY. AND IT'S YOURS. YOU JUST HAVE TO FIND IT.

WE WILL. THANK YOU.
WE LOVE YOU SO MUCH, VI.

"BE FOREWARNED, MY SISTERS--
I LEFT THE WEAPON ON THE
HIGHEST PEAK OF THE TALLEST
MOUNTAIN IN THE WHOLE REALM."
"IT IS THE MOST DANGEROUS
THING YOU COULD POSSIBLY
WIELD, BUT THE JOURNEY TO
GET IT? EVEN MORE SO."
N
"THIS WILL BE THE HARDEST
THING YOU'VE EVER DONE.
BUT I PROMISE YOU, IT WILL
BE WORTH IT."

YOU... WHAT? YOU LET THEM ESCAPE?
TH-THEY BLINDSIDED US. WE WERE V-VIGILANT. THE BATTLE WAS--
tonight PRIVATE EVENT

YOU LET THE RAT FUCKING QUEENS GET AWAY FROM ME?!

SHIK

GAHH! PLEASE, MY LORD! I JUST WANT TO DAN--
SHUNK

SHUNK
SHUNK
SHUNK

AUGHHHHHH!!!
KOFF

SQLURCH
THANK YOU, PROFESSOR FUDGE. THANK YOU.
AHH, YOU CALM ME DOWN, MY ONLY FRIEND.

OKAY. IT'S FINE, IT'S ALL FINE. THIS IS TOTALLY FIXABLE. NO PROBLEM. WE GOT THIS. ALL GOOD.
SO. HERE'S WHAT WE'RE GONNA DO, Y'ALL...

"...OTHER GARY AND OTHER OTHER GARY--I WANT YOU TO FORM A DEATH SQUAD. HUNT THE RAT QUEENS."
"WHEREVER THEY'VE BEEN, WHEREVER THEY ARE. FLUSH THEM OUT. BRING THEM TO ME."
"I WANT THEM TO WATCH ME SLAUGHTER EVERYONE THEY'VE EVER KNOWN."

CHAPTER EIGHTEEN

he Soul Shadow
lountains.
"THAT'S IT-- I'M *DEAD.*"

I'M ABSOLUTELY DEAD, BRAGA. THIS IS SOME SICK DEATH DREAM...A TERRIBLE AFTERLIFE. THIS HAS TO BE HELL.
SAVE YOUR STRENGTH, MADDIE. YOU'RE JUST COLD...AND BEING CARRIED. IT COULD BE WORSE.
WE'RE NOT FAR. I THINK. PAST THE POINT OF RETURN, ANYWAYS.
SO...SO HOT, TERWILLIGER. SWEAT...SOAKING ME...LIKE DEW ON A COLD PINT GLASS...
YOU EVEN *THINK* OF DRINKING AND I'LL KILL YA MYSELF, THEN HAUNT YER DRUNK ASS IN THE NEXT LIFE.

HANNAH. I WANT TO TALK... BURY THE HATCHET.
YOU'VE ALREADY BURIED ENOUGH HATCHETS IN OUR BACKS. IF WE GET OUT OF THIS ALIVE, I'LL GIVE YOU A MINUTE FOR EACH FINGER I HAVE LEFT.
YOU DON'T UNDERSTAND--
IT'S TOO COLD FOR THIS, DEE...

"...OR DO YOU NOT FEEL WHAT US *MERE MORTALS* DO?"
IS THAT AN--
ICE BRIDGE.
AND ARE WE...
YEAH. WE *ARE.*
NO MORE FREE RIDE, MADS.

EASY. GET AS LOW AS YOU CAN TO THE ICE--KEEP YOUR WEIGHT SPREAD OUT BEST YOU CAN.
IT'S NOT GONNA BREAK, IT'S NOT GONNA BREAK, IT'S NOT GONNA BREAK...
REMIND ME TO SEND VIOLET A LOVELY BOUQUET OF MIDDLE FINGERS IF WE MAKE IT.
WE--WE'RE OVER HALFWAY NOW! THIS BRIDGE IS SOLID! WE CAN MAKE--
DEFENSIVE POSITIONS!
WAIT, WHAT?
FUCK. FUCK FUCK FUCK!
HURRY! AS FAST AS YOU CAN, ARM YOURSELVES!
HOH THERE! RAT QUEENS, I ASSUME?
KING GARY SENDS HIS REGARDS.
AND HIS DEATH SQUAD, HAH HAH!
'FRAID HE SENT US TO KILL YA'S DEAD.
CAN'T OUTRUN THE KING, LADIES.
MOVE! I'M GONNA PUKE!
SAVE YERSELF, BETTY! DON'T LET THESE ENABLERS DRAG YA DOWN!

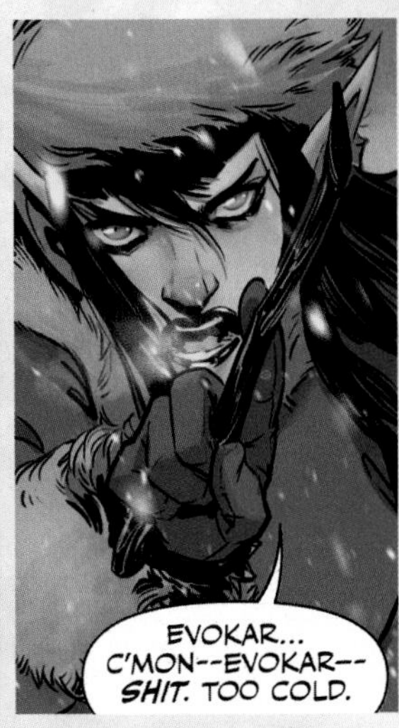
EVOKAR... C'MON--EVOKAR-- SHIT. TOO COLD.

OH NO.
IT'S GONNA BREAK, IT'S GONNA BREAK, IT'S GONNA--
KRRRK

THWIP
THWIP
THWIP

SHUNK
SHUNK
AUGHH!!
GO! HURRY!

BRAGA!
SHIT! SHIT SHIT SHIT!

WUH-OH.
WE'RE GONNA HAVE TO WORK ON YER COPING MECHANISMS, DOLL.

HRRG

...JUST... HOLD ON...
MADDIE, STAY WHERE YOU ARE!
OW! HEY!

I GOT YOU...I THINK?
YOU'RE DOING FABULOUS, BRAGA. PLEASE KEEP IT UP.
I THINK... I THINK I CAN DO IT...

ALL RIGHT, YOU...YOU...DUMB... YOU DUMB... FF-FUCKS!
MADDIE! GET BACK! I'LL HRRN BE RIGHT THERE!

THE SMALL ONES ALWAYS EITHER RUN AWAY FIRST OR THINK THEY'RE THE BIGGEST. LIKE, EVERY TIME.
THEY SPLAT THE MOST THOUGH. IT'S WEIRDLY THERAPEUTIC.

NGULP

HANNAH! DEE! DO SOMETHING!
LOOK AT YOU. NO WONDER YER A BOOZEHOUND. NO PRIDE. TOTALLY SELFISH.
YER THE SMALLEST. YOU COULD'VE JUMPED UP THERE AN' FOUGHT THEM. MAYBE COULD'VE TAKEN THEM.
BUT...BUT YOU--
"A LESSON, THIS--AN' THE BEST ONES ARE USUALLY THE HARDEST."
HOW THE ≈HUFF≈ HELL ARE YOU TWO SO HEAVY!
DON'T LOOK AT ME, I LOST A COUPLE POUNDS
IT'S ME. WITHIN ME IS THE WEIGHT OF A HUNDRED REALMS.
I'VE IGNORED IT FOR TOO LONG. HURT THE ONES I LOVE.
NO. MORE.
DEE...
HOLY FUCK, SHE'S ACTUALLY DOING IT.

LIKE SHOOTING A FLOATY FISH IN A NET...
C'MON, SCOOTER! LET ME HAVE THIS ONE!
DON'T TOUCH MY FRIENDS.

SHRAK
SKYLAR!
SKYLAR, ARE YOU OKAY?!

YOU HAVE NO IDEA WHO YOU'VE MESSED WITH. I'M GOING TO TURN YOUR--
DEE. YOU ARE TEMPTING SOMETHING.
WHAT...WHAT IN GODS...WHAT'S HAPPENING?
THE CONSEQUENCES OF WHICH YOU DO NOT COMPREHEND.

THIS IS A WARNING, DEE OF PALISADE. YOU ARE NOT AUTHORIZED TO USE YOUR POWERS INDUED. YOU ARE BUT A... CLERICAL ERROR.
YOUR INSTINCTS WERE CORRECT. MEDDLE NOT WITH THE MORTALS, SHOULD YOU NOT WISH TO INCITE A REIGN OF VIOLENCE AND WAR THE LIKES OF WHICH ANY REALM HAS NEVER SEEN.

TAKE GOOD FUCKING HEED.
I KNEW IT. I CAN'T.
I CAN'T DO IT!

I WILL AVENGE YOU, SKYLARRRRRRRRRRRR!

OH FUCK.
DEE? GODSDAMN FINISH IT!
WHAT AM I?

I'M N-NOT BACKING DOWN. I'M N-NOT A GOD...

...I'M M-MADELINE.

THWUMP

OOOOF. NICE.

SNFF SKYLAR WOULD'VE LOVED THA--

CRACK

HOLD STILL, TERWILLIGER! I'M NOT DONE STABBING.

YOU. THIS IS ON YOU. YOU DANGLED THE CARROT. ALMOST ACTED LIKE A SISTER. AND THEN...
...YOU FUCKING COWARD.
WHEN I STARTED USING MY POWERS ***SOMETHING HAPPENED***... SOMETHING VERY, ***VERY*** BAD.

"WHATEVER IT IS, IT DOESN'T MATTER, DEE--YOU JUST DID THE WORST THING."
SHE'S ALIVE. I'M GOING TO FIND HER.
BRAGA... EVEN YOU COULDN'T HAVE SURVIVED THAT IMPACT. THAT FALL. THIS COLD.
YOU'VE HAD THAT THIS WHOLE TIME?!
DO NOT DO THIS NOW. I NEED THIS.
NONE OF US ARE DEATH-PROOF. ANY TIME, ANY OF THESE QUESTS, THAT COULD'VE BEEN ME. OR YOU. OR BETTY.
SHE WAS...TOO NEW.
SHE IS ONE OF US. SHE HAS HEART.
SHE'S MY RESPONSIBILITY. SHE'S...
...SHE'S GONE.
YOU KNOW WHAT WE HAVE TO DO NOW. ALL YOUR RAGE, ALL YOUR PAIN, BRAGA--HOLD IT FOR GARY.
LET'S FIND VIOLET'S WEAPON AND GET THE HECK OUT OF HERE...

"...AND GET BACK HOME. TO PALISADE. IF THERE'S ANYTHING LEFT."
YES, YESSS! PROSPER! LIFE IS GOOD, YOU CUNTS!

I AM YOUR KING! YOU LOVE ME, ALL OF YOU DO! WE WILL CELEBRATE THAT! WITH A PARADE! *TRI-WEEKLY,* HENCEFORTH!
UGH, WHAT A PRICK. WE GOTTA DO THIS THREE TIMES A WEEK? OR WAIT, IS THAT ONCE EVERY THREE WEEKS?
HEY! KING DICKHEAD! WHAT'S TRI-WEEKLY MEAN? THIS IS BULLSHIT!
SHUT IT, PLEB! SHOW YOUR HIGHNESS SOME DING DANG RESPECT!

YES, YES, SEE, YOU ALL HAVE A VOICE HERE, IN THIS NEW KINGDOM.
AND I HAVE THE UNWAVERING RIGHT TO KNOCK YOUR TEETH DOWN YOUR THROAT FOR SAYING SOMETHING DUMB.
SEE?! FREEDOM! YOU CAN SAY ANYTHING YOU WANT AND IT SHALL ELICIT AN APPROPRIATE REACTION!
THERE'S NO TYRANNY HERE! I'M FUCKING BENEVOLENT AND STRONG.

WELCOME, CITIZENS OF MY KINGDOM, TO THE INAUGURAL CELEBRATION OF OUR HOME. PALISADE NO MORE, BOTH IN OPERATION AND IN NAME.
YOUR NEW HOME...

...GARY.

GOOD LORDS, THIS ASSHOLE RENAMED THE CITY AFTER HIMSELF?!
HEY, FUCK YOU.
AH-HEM. LISTEN, LIFE IN GARY IS GOING TO BE WICKED.

SAFETY? YOU GOT IT. AIN'T NO ONE MESSING WITH THIS ARMY, AND THAT'S A FACT, JACK. HEALTHCARE? UNIVERSAL. EVERYONE GETS COVERAGE--FOR FREE. FUCK A GERM.
LOCAL BUSINESS ONLY. YOU WANNA WORK? NO PROBLEMO. DON'T WANNA WORK? PUT AN EGG IN YOUR SHOE AND BEAT IT.

ALL I DEMAND IS YOUR ENDLESS, UNWAVERING OBEDIENCE. LIKE, LITERALLY.
BULLLLSHIT. PALISADE NEEDS YOU LIKE I NEED A BUTTHOLE ON MY FOREHEAD.

YOU--THE BIGGEST, LAMEST PIECE OF ENTITLED, ANNOYING SHIT--TUCKED YOUR LITTLE, TINY BALLS BETWEEN YOUR MILKY-WHITE THIGHS AND LEFT THIS PLACE.
AND NOW YOU'RE BACK WITH A SHITTY GRUDGE AND SOME MUSCLE, BUT REALLY ONLY ONE THING IS CERTAIN HERE...

...YOU ARE REMARKABLE. EVERYONE KNOWS YOU'RE OF NO USE. TO ANYONE. EVER.

GO ON THEN! TELL US WHAT YOU THINK! WE'RE ALL LISTENING!
YOU HAVE YOUR KING'S ATTENTION, HAHAHA!
THWAK
AUGHHHHHH!!!

FINALLY, SOME FREAKING SHELTER. THIS COLD IS KILLING M--ERR, NOT AGREEING WITH ME.
ONE SECOND YOU'RE HOT, THE NEXT YOU'RE COLD. PICK ONE.
NOT A VERY GOOD SUPPORT SYSTEM, ARE YA? SHE'S YOUR FRIEND, PAL.
GIMME A BREAK--WE ALL ARE. ALSO, I MADE YOU. I CAN UN-MAKE YOU.
HANNAH! DON'T TALK TO MY CARING DAUGHTER LIKE THAT.
WHOA WHOA WHOA... I'M NOT YOUR DAUGH--
SNFF SNFF HOLD.
HANNAH. LIGHT?

EVOKAR ILLUMINUS.
BZZZT
HEY, LOOK! IT WORKED! HAH! NICE!

RAHHHH!
OH. MY. GODS. IT'S A **SNOGRE!** I THOUGHT THEY ALL DIED!
YEAH, NO SHIT. I DONATED TO THAT SNOGRE CHARITY ONCE.
HEY! SNOGRE! YOU OWE ME SOME COIN--YOU AREN'T DEAD!
KUURRRRR...
LISTEN UP, BUTTERCUP. WE ESCAPED PRISON. TRAVELLED FOR A WEEK THROUGH THESE MOUNTAINS. IT'S COLD AS HELL. WE'RE TIRED. OUR SISTER WAS JUST ***MURDERED.***

I CAN SEE YOU'RE ONLY PROTECTING YOUR BABIES...BUT WE JUST WANT ***PASSAGE.*** I WILL IGNORE EVERY IMPULSE IN ME TO NOT RUN THROUGH YOU TO GET OUT OF THIS CAVE.

GGRRARRGHH--

HAHA, I'M ONLY FUCKIN' WITH YA--JUST CHILL.
GET IT? ***CHILL?*** SNOW CAVE, COLD, ET CETERA.

OH MY GODS, THANK YOU. I DON'T KNOW WHAT ANIMAL THIS IS, BUT THAT'S A SPECIES I'D EAT TO EXTINCTION.
WHOOOA. LITTLE CLOSE TO HOME THERE.
SHIT, SORRY.
NOW WE'RE EVEN FOR THE DONATION, HAH.
DIDN'T SEE A COIN FROM THAT. THOSE CHARITIES ARE SCAMS.

YOU'RE REALLY THE LAST OF YOUR KIND? I'M SORRY.
IT MUST BE HARD, NOT KNOWING HOW AND WHERE TO FIT.

I MEAN, KINDA. MY KIND JUST KEPT TO OURSELVES MOSTLY. WE WERE FINE UNTIL OTHER FOLKS GOT CLOSER AND CLOSER.
SO WE HAD TO GO HIGHER AND HIGHER, AND EVENTUALLY...

"LUCKILY, BEFORE MY MATE SUCCUMBED TO THE HARSH PERILS OF THE ASCENT, I SHOT MY BEANS UP HER MUFF."

LIFE FINDS A WAY, EH? HAH!
YOU GALS DID PRETTY GOOD THOUGH. KUDOS. YOU'RE WELCOME TO CRASH HERE FOR A BIT.
WE APPRECIATE THAT...

"...BUT WE'RE ON A MISSION TO SAVE *OUR* KIND."
HUFF HUFF
THIS...IS WILDLY UNNECESSARY?
NICE.
JUST LET HER DO IT. THIS IS FINE.

THERE.

KSH
ABOUT TIME...

...I WAS WONDERING HOW IN THE HECK I WAS GONNA GET *BACK DOWN* FROM HERE.

MADDIE?!
BUT... HOW?

WELLLL, IT HURT LIKE CRAZY, BUT I BOUNCED. THE HAMMER GUY WHACKED ME AND I FLEW INTO THE OTHER MOUNTAIN AND BOUNCED OFF *THAT* AND I THOUGHT I WAS GONNA SINK LIKE A ROCK BUT I FLEW EVEN HIGHER AND LANDED--

BRAGA, I'M SORRY. I DIDN'T LISTEN... I SHOULD--
YOU DID GOOD, QUEEN.

REAL DAMN GOOD.

THERE'S *THAT* THING. IT'S ALL THAT'S BEEN UP HERE. I HAVEN'T OPENED IT.
MUST BE VIOLET'S SECRET SUPERWEAPON?
HUH. A BOX. THOUGHT IT WOULD BE, LIKE, A MAGICAL FLAMING SWORD OR SOMETHING.
JUST WHAT HAVE YOU SENT US HERE FOR, VI?

NO WAY.
I DON'T UNDERSTAND? WHERE'S THE WEAPON?
OH WOW.
HAHA! COOOOL!

IT LOOKS LIKE A...
...IT'S A *TIME CAPSULE*.
THE SCROLL. READ IT.

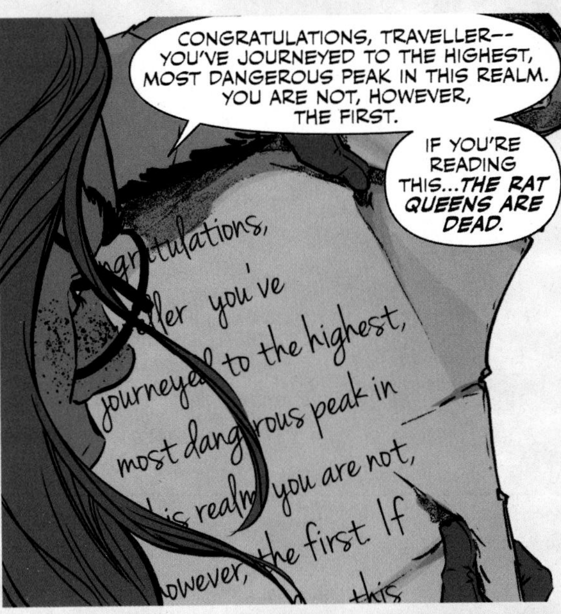
CONGRATULATIONS, TRAVELLER-- YOU'VE JOURNEYED TO THE HIGHEST, MOST DANGEROUS PEAK IN THIS REALM. YOU ARE NOT, HOWEVER, THE FIRST.
IF YOU'RE READING THIS...*THE RAT QUEENS ARE DEAD*.
to the highest,
most dang rous peak in
you are not,
the first. If

THEY WERE THE FIRST TO REACH THE TOP OF THIS MOUNTAIN. THIS IS THEIR STORY. THEIR LEGACY.
BUT, WE *WEREN'T* THE FIRST.

VIOLET WAS. SHE'S A RAT QUEEN. AND NOW WE'RE HERE. SO, TECHNICALLY...
...SHIT, Y'ALL. WE CONQUERED THIS. THIS MOUNTAIN IS OURS.

"THEY WERE FEARLESS. THEIR BRAVERY HAD NO END. THEY WERE MISUNDERSTOOD. THEY WERE SISTERS."

THIS SAYS IT'S FOR *YOU*, HANNAH. AND THERE'S A NOTE.
My dear Hannah. You don't need this to be good. You already are. I just thought it would look great.
P.S. maybe don't diddle with it.
VIOLET, YOU BEAUTIFUL BASTARD.

THIS ONE'S FOR--WAIT... *FOR ME?!*
Maddie, this is for you to have now. Earn it. Deserve it. And know that you have every right to it.
OOH, WHAT IS THAT? IS IT A *CUP*? LET'S FILL IT! I'M *PARCHED*.
NO, BETTY. YOU DON'T NEED TO.
IT'S DAVE'S *BATTLE HORN*. FOR *ALL* OF US TO HAVE.

DO WE JUST...LEAVE THE CHEST HERE?
VIOLET'S RIGHT--SOME DAY *WE WON'T* BE HERE...
BUT *THIS* WILL. A *LEGACY*. LET'S LEAVE IT.
FOR THE *SECOND-BEST* BUNCH OF BADASSES TO FIND.

Atop this peak is the greatest weapon of all. Stronger than iron. Sharper than any blade. Hotter than any fire.
Your hands. Your eyes. You.
Surround yourself with love. Open your hearts. Breathe the same air. Feel with every inch of your body and mind.
Form an unbreakable bond that no army can ever overpower.
Be indestructible in your souls.
Have fun.
Eternally grateful and proud,
Violet Blackforge

ByOOOOO

OOOOOOOO
NGUH! DEBATE ME!
MM. BAD DREAM. NIGHTLIGHT.

OOOOOOOO

AY! I'M TRYIN' TO GET MY BEAUTY REST HERE!
THIS IS MY KINGDOM--I MAKE THE BIG FUN SOUNDS, SHUT YOUR--
WAKE UP, PALISADE!

RISE 'N SHINE, BITCHES--THE RAT QUEENS ARE HOME.

CHAPTER NINETEEN

GARY! WE SEE YOU UP THERE! YOU LOOK LIKE AN UPRIGHT FROG!
PUT SOME CLOTHES ON, FOR THE LOVE OF GODS. THEN GET YOUR PIMPLY LITTLE ASS DOWN HERE!
WHAT THE HELL? I SENT A DEATH SQUAD AFTER YOU!

YOUR SHITTY INVASION IS OVER, AND WE AIN'T FUCKIN' AROUND THIS TIME, BUCK-O!
YOU CAN EITHER TURN YOURSELF IN FOR BANISHMENT TO THE DARKEST REALM OF MY CHOOSING...
...OR EVERYONE IN PALISADE GETS A TURN FOOT-FUCKING YOUR TOOTHLESS MOUTH WHILE BRAGA DIGS A BIG OL' HOLE TO BURY YOU AND YOUR DICK-STAIN FRIENDS.

THEN WE'LL SALT THE EARTH AND EVERYONE IN TOWN'S GONNA BLAST PISS ON IT! NOTHING SHALL EVER GROW THERE AGAIN!

AND WE'LL MARK THE SPOT WITH A BIIIG STATUE OF YOUR MOUTH-BREATHING, PISS-DRINKING FACE WITH A SHINY PLAQUE THAT READS, "HERE LIES GARY, THE BIGGEST ASSHOLE IN ANY LAND."
AND I'LL SHINE THAT BAD BOY UP EVERY DAMN DAY, FOR EVERYONE TO SEE, WHILE I CONTINUE VOIDING MY BLADDER ON YOUR ROTTING BONES!

WHOA.
HANNAH, THAT WAS...
EW.

NO!
I WILL NEVER BE FORCED TO DRINK PISS!
THIS IS BULLSHIT! SERIOUSLY! GODS!

GALS? I'M FEELING SOMETHING...ODD. LIKE... WORRIED? NORMALLY THIS WOULD BE FUN FOR ME...RIGHT?
IT'S CALLED SOBRIETY, GENIUS. DEAL.
BRAGA? ANY ADVICE?
NAH, NOT ANYMORE, DOLL...
...JUST SWING AWAY ON THESE ASSHOLES.
--THE FUCK ARE YA DOING? GET UP! THEY NEED YA! YOUR SISTERS NEED YA, YA PRICK!
I CAN'T, TERWILLIGER...I JUST CAN'T. THIS IS INSANE.
I HATE THIS! THIS IS TERRIFYING!
HEY, LOOK! CAUGHT ME A FAIRY!
PLUCK
ACK! AVENGE ME! I'M YER DAUGHTER, FOR GODS' SAKE!
CRAP CRAP CRAP CRAAAP...

BZZZZT
EVOKAR RETINUS!
HAH! HOLY HELL, I'M BACK, BITCHES!

THWAK

HRRN!

OH MY GOODNESS--LOOK! GUYS! I GOT A TWO-FER!
SHIK

HEY... ANYONE SEEN BETTY?
SHE'S ALWAYS LOVED A GOOD BUTT WHOOPIN'...

PAR PA PRAAAAP
THE RIGHT HONOURABLE KING GARY HAS SUMMONED HIS PRECIOUS!
PROFESSOR CORNELIUS FUDGEBOTTOM III HAS ENTERED THE BATTLEFIELD!
BWOOF
LORDS TAKE PITY ON ANY SOUL CAUGHT IN THE BEAST'S MOIST AND WANTING FLAPPERS!
EASY NOW! EEEASY, BIG FELLA!
HUFF GNORT
I HATE TO DO THIS, MADDIE, BUT YOU'RE THE NEWBIE. SSSOOO...
YEAH...
SO? SO WHAT? WAIT--
...YOU GOTTA GO KILL THAT CUTE-ASS DOG.
GASP

I CAN'T DO IT, HANNAH. I JUST--
RAT QUEENS NEVER SAY "CAN'T," MADDIE. YOU THINK I GOT TO WHERE I AM BY NOT SLAYING SOME CUTIE PIES?

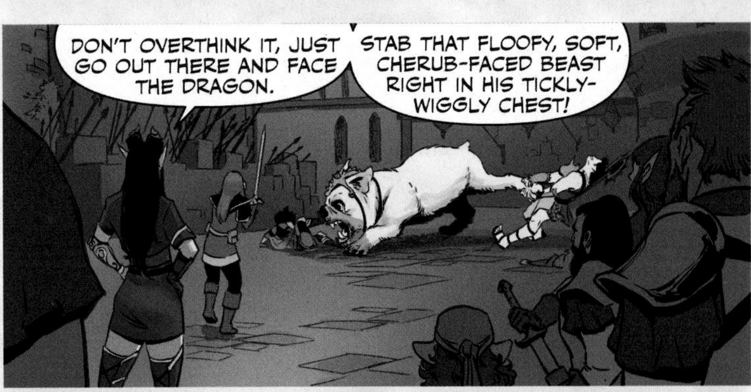
DON'T OVERTHINK IT, JUST GO OUT THERE AND FACE THE DRAGON.
STAB THAT FLOOFY, SOFT, CHERUB-FACED BEAST RIGHT IN HIS TICKLY-WIGGLY CHEST!

BAHAHA! LOOK AT 'IM GO! ATTA BOY, DOGGO!
THEY AIN'T GOT A FRIGGIN' CHANCE AGAINST OL' FUDGE.

HOLD UP, HOLD UP, JUST HOLD UP HERE...
SHE'S... SHE'S NOT GONNA...*IS SHE?*

SHE'S GONNA *KILL* THAT DOG! *A DOG!* SHE CAN'T DO THAT!
OH HOHOHO NO. I CAN'T LOOK. PURE EVIL.

I-I...I'M S-SORRY, P-PROFESSOR F-FUDGE ≈SNIFF≈...
...SH-SHE T-TOLD ME ≈HFF HFF≈ I H-HAVE TO!
Y-YOU'RE SOOO C-CUUUTE ≈UHHH≈

DON'T YOU FREAKING DARE!

YOU EVEN *THINK* ABOUT TOUCHING MY FUR BABY AND I PUT THIS KNIFE THROUGH DRUNKY'S LITTLE EARHOLE.
GOOD NEWS, EVERYONE... ƎHCKƐ MAESTRO'S HAS AN ƎHCKƐ OPEN BAR...
I DUNNO WHERE ƎHCKƐ TERWILLIGER WENT, BUT ƎHCKƐ MAN, SHE WAS A BUZZ-KILL, AMIRITE, HAAH...

AW, BETTY. NO.
N'RYGOTH MCFUCK-BUTTER.
IT WAS BOUND TO HAPPEN. MAYBE. WE HAVE TO GO EASY ON HER.

HEYYY, ANY'A YOUS WANNA SPLIT A PIZZ-- *UURRGGL!*
GAHH! GET HER AWAY FROM ME! THIS ROBE IS PURE VENUVIAN SPIDER SILK!
YOU. YOU JUST HAAAD TO KEEP TWISTIN' MY NIPS, DIDN'T YOU?

HOW DO YOU THINK THIS IS GOING TO PLAY OUT? WE'RE JUST GOING TO LET YOU TAKE OVER PALISADE?
YOU THINK WE'D JUST LET YOU LOCK US UP AND NOT DO ANYTHING ABOUT IT? YOU KNOW WHO WE ARE--WHAT WE DO.

WELL, IT'S PLAYED OUT THUS FAR WITH YOU, ONCE AGAIN, IN A POSITION TO DO *JACK SHIT.*
THIS TIME, I'M MAKING *SURE.* NO MORE OF YOUR RAT QUEENS BULLHONKY.

WE RUSH THEM ON THE COUNT OF THREE.
NO. HE'LL *KILL BETTY.* HE TALKS A LOT, BUT WE CAN'T RISK IT.
IT WAS A GOOD COMEBACK, ALBEIT BRIEF, I GUESS.
YOU TRY TO KILL MY DOG?
N-NO. I C-COULDN'T.
I KNOW. PROFESSOR FUDGE IS *UNSTOPPABLE.*
WHO EVEN *ARE* YOU?
Y-YOU ASKED ME THAT ALREADY. M-MY NAME'S M-MADD--

THUD
DON'T CARE! YOU'RE NO ONE! SCARING MY DOG LIKE THAT--*FUCK YOU!*
TAKE THAT WANNABE, OFF-BRAND VIOLET OUT OF HERE! THROW HER ASS IN A BOG FOR ALL I CARE!
THE *REAL* RAT QUEENS ARE THE ONES I WANT.
NO MORE BLUFFING. NO MORE FALSE STARTS. NO MORE GAMES...

"...Y'ALL ARE SERIOUSLY EFFED THIS TIME."
BANG
ORDER! ORDER IN THE COURT!
ZIP IT, I'M TRYING TO TALK HERE! C'MONNN!
AH-HEM
DEARLY BELOVEDS, WE ARE GATHERED HERE TODAY, IN THIS MOST RESPECTED SUPREME COURT OF NEW GARY--FORMERLY "PALISADE"--TO WITNESS THE COMING OF JUSTICE TO WHAT COULD BE THIS REALM'S MOST IRRITABLE PESTS.
WELCOME TO THE TRIAL OF THE RAT QUEENS!

HRNN
OH GODS... I BLACKED OUT FOR A WHILE THERE--I NEED TERWILLIGER. BAD.
I THINK WE'RE DOING ONE OF THOSE "THIS IS YOUR LIFE" THINGS. SOOO...WE'RE FUCKED.
DEE, IS IT EVEN WORTH ASKING TO PULL THE GOD CARD ANYMORE?
IT'S MORE THAN A MORAL CHOICE NOW, HANNAH. SOMETHING WARNED ME ON THAT ICE BRIDGE...

SILENCE! THE ACCUSED WILL SHUT THEIR PIE HOLES!
NOW HEAR YE THIS--AND THIS GOES TO ALL YE BITCHES IN MY COURT--I MAY BE STERN, YES, BUT I AM FAIR.

I WILL ALLOW YOU BRAT QUEEFS TO REPRESENT YOURSELVES IN THIS COURT AND PLEAD YOUR CASES. I WILL ALSO ALLOW TESTIMONIAL FROM THOSE NEW GARYANS WILLING.
WHO AM I KIDDING? THIS COULD BE *ACTUALLY HILARIOUS.*

OBJECTION! THIS IS PURE LUNACY! UTTER PIG SPITTLE! THEY'VE DONE NOTHING! FOR WHAT CRIMES ARE THEY CHARGED?
YOU'RE JUST A BITTER IDIOT WITH A PERSONAL BONE TO PICK.
WHERE'S MY DAUGHTER? YOU'RE A DEAD MAN, YOU ASS--

HAAH! THAT'S RICH. SHUT IT, INMATES! DON'T YOU FORGET THAT YOU'RE *NEXT* ON THE STAND.
I TAKE IMMENSE JOY IN HAVING YOU TREASONOUS SWINE IN MY AUDIENCE.

ALL RIGHTY THEN, LET'S GET THIS SHOW ON THE ROAD-- *COURT IS IN SESSION!*
WE WILL NOW PERMIT THE DEFENDANTS' OPENING STATEMENTS. MAKE 'EM GOOD, THIS IS THE ONLY CHANCE YOU GET.

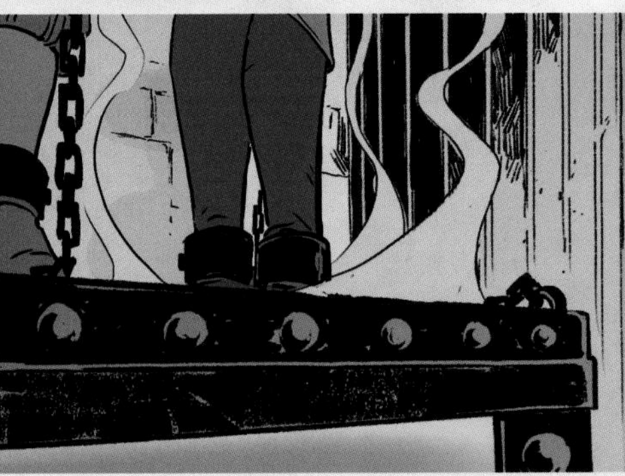

THIS IS INSANE.
LOOK, I DON'T WANT TO SOUND OVER-CONFIDENT, BUT I THINK I CAN LAWYER US OUT OF THIS.
YOU'RE STILL DRUNK, SMIDGEON. I'LL DO THE TALKING. I'VE GOT A FEW NUGGETS OF TRUTH I'D LIKE TO LAY ON KING ASSFACE.

OKAY, BUT DON'T PISS HIM--
YOUR HONOUR...PEOPLE OF THE COURT... HUMBLE DENIZENS OF PALISADE...MAY THE RECORD SHOW THAT GARY IS **NOT** AN ASSHOLE.
HE'S A BIG OL' ***BITCH!***

YOU THINK THIS IS GOING TO STAND? YOU THINK THIS IS JUSTICE? JUSTICE FOR WHAT?
EVERYONE IN PALISADE KNOWS YOU'RE A DELICATE, FRAGILE, EGO-DRIVEN BOTTOM FEEDER WITH MEDIOCRE LUCK.
YOU, GARRRY, ARE LUCKY YOU MADE IT A DAY OUT OF THE WOMB, LET ALONE A DAY IN PALISADE THE FIRST TIME YOU SHOWED UP AND STUNK THE PLACE TO HIGH HEAVENS.
YOU WERE A BUMMER THEN AND AN EVEN BIGGER BITCH NOW, AND GUESS WHAT, DICK-NECK? LUCK WON'T GET YOU TOO FAR FOR TOO LONG.

ALSO, YOU SMELL LIKE ONIONS AND YOUR TEETH LOOK LIKE CORN.
THE DEFENCE RESTS. BITCH.

HOH-KAY, MOVING ON...
...THE COURT WOULD LIKE TO CALL SOME CITIZENS OF NEW GARY TO THE STAND SO WE CAN HEAR THEIR TESTIMONY.

THEY MAGIC-BAGGED ME! STOLE SEVERAL FUCKIN' CUPCAKES!

ONCE THERE WAS A SHIT IN MY SHOE--HAD TO BE THE LITTLE ONE.

zzzZZzz

CHARGE TOO MUCH. UNPROFESSIONAL. WOULDN'T HIRE.

I SAW 'EM MURDER A CHILD!
YOU PROMISED ME A SANDWI--

BROKE MY DAMN HEART. ALL OF 'EM.

SHE HID IN A PRESENT... AND STABBED MY EYES OUT!

USED TO TURN ME ON MY SHELL AND WATCH ME SQUIRM ALL ABOUT. FOR THE *LAUGHS* OF IT.

THE RAT QUEENS? THEY BRING DEATH AND DESTRUCTION TO ***EVERYTHING.***

THAT WAS...
...SOBERING.
I DON'T REMEMBER MURDERING A CHILD?
WHEN YOU PUT IT ALL TOGETHER LIKE THAT, IT REALLY DOESN'T FEEL GREAT.
WOW. HOW POWERFUL WAS THAT?
THESE PEOPLE, HERE TODAY TO SPEAK THEIR TRUTH, ARE HEROES.
THIS COURT HONOURS YOU.
WELL, THAT'S ALL I NEEDED TO HEAR!
HOW ABOUT WE MAKE LIKE A DONKEY DINK AND "HIT THE ROAD" WITH THE FORMALITIES, HUH?
ONTO MY JUDGEMENT!
HE'S LOCKED US IN REAL GOOD HERE.
IT'S ALL ENCHANTED, LIKE THE PRISON.
WAIT!
YOU'RE A SMART GUY, GARY. GIVE US SOMETHING. ONE LAST SHOT AT A DEFENCE. YOU SAID YOURSELF, YOU'RE A BENEVOLENT RULER...
HMMM.
I'LL TELL YOU WHAT...I'LL PARDON YOU COMPLETELY--BUT ONLY IF...

...YOU CAN NAME ONE GOOD THING ABOUT ME.

GO ON THEN. I'LL GIVE YOU A MINUTE.

WE HAD A GOOD RUN, MY FRIENDS.
WAIT... ONE THING? ABOUT HIM?
I MEAN... SHIT. HE'S KINDA...

...HE'S KINDA--OH GODS, I CAN'T BELIEVE I'M SAYING THIS-- FUCKABLE?
LIKE, HEAR ME OUT. I WOULDN'T GO OUT OF MY WAY TO FUCK HIM. BUT IF IT WAS ONE OF "THOSE NIGHTS" AND LITERALLY EVERYONE IN PALISADE DIED OR HAD COCK-ROT...
...MAYYYBE I'D LET HIM SMASH--UHHHH, NO NO NO...

MAYBE IF HE WERE THE ONLY OPTION, AND IF BOTH OF MY HANDS WERE GONE--I'M TALKING LIVING POTATO HEAD ON A PILLOW TYPE THING HERE...
...AND IF IT TURNED OUT GARY WAS ONE OF THOSE WEIRD, SKINNY HALF-WITS BUT, LIKE, WEIRDLY HUNG LIKE A RHINOPHANT...

NO. NUH UH. STILL NO. COULDN'T DO IT.
SORRY, Y'ALL. I GOT NOTHING.

≈KOFF KOFF≈

NOT. EVEN. FUCKABLE.
EVEN FOR A LIVING POTATO HEAD ON A PILLOW.

BRAGA...
...BETTY...
...HANNAH...
...DEE...
...I DON'T KNOW YOUR FRIGGIN' LAST NAMES...

...I FIND YOU GUILTY OF THE CRIME OF BEING THE ABSOLUTE SHITS AND THE BIGGEST PAIN IN MY ASS FOR AS LONG AS THIS REALM HAS EVER KNOWN!

I HEREBY SENTENCE YOU, RAT QUEENS... TO DEATH!
HORRIBLE, PAINFUL, IRREVERSIBLE, IMMEDIATE DEATH!

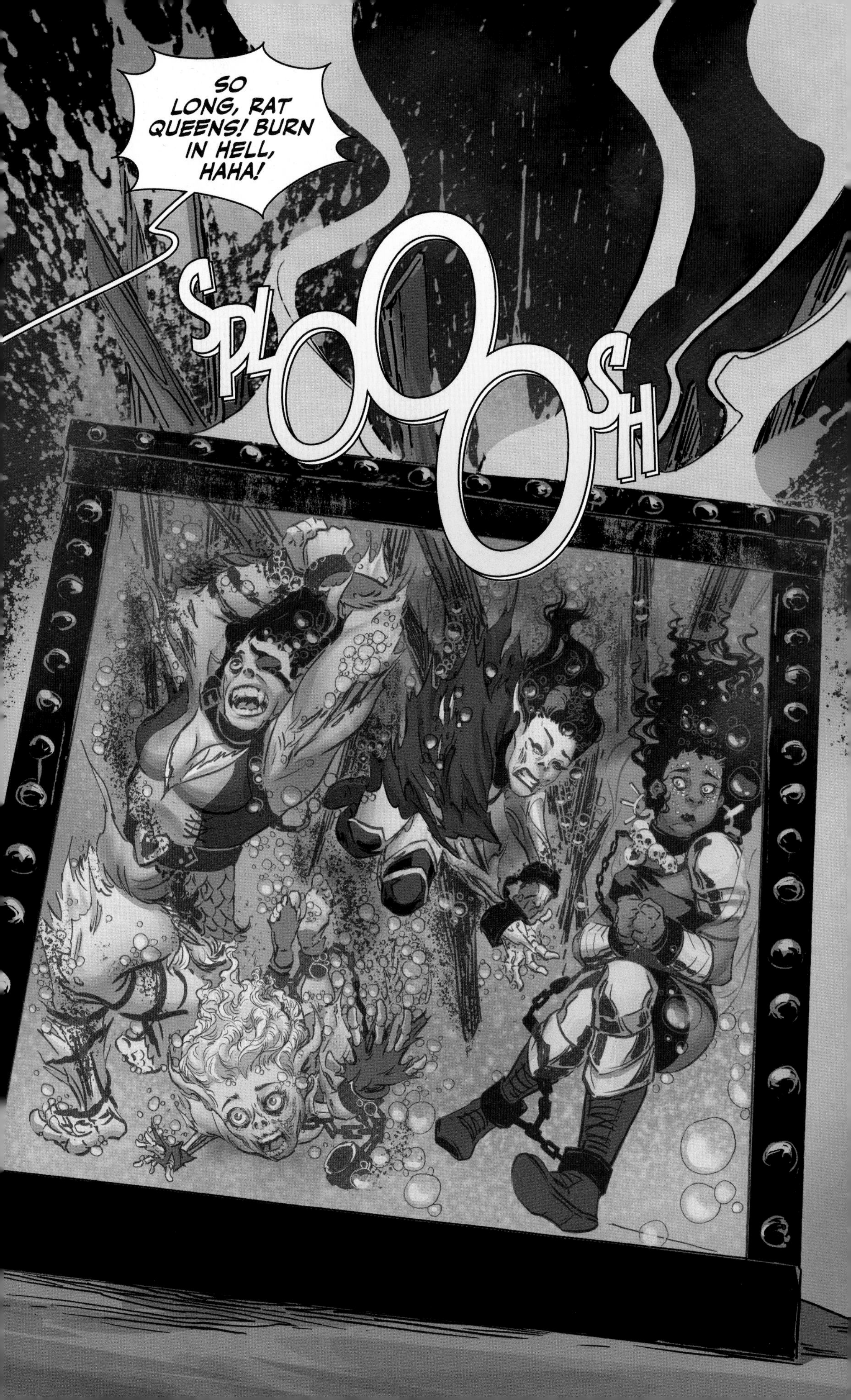
SO LONG, RAT QUEENS! BURN IN HELL, HAHA!
SPLOOOSH

NO.
NO!
DID I NOT TELL YOU ONCE BEFORE, DEE?
DID I NOT WARN YOU OF THE SEVERITY OF WHAT WILL HAPPEN WHEN YOU MEDDLE WITH THEM?
YOU KNOW NOT WHAT YOU'RE DOING, NOR THE MAGNITUDE OF THE POWER YOU POSSESS...

...BUT I ASSURE YOU, THE CONSEQUENCES ARE VERY MUCH MORE DEVASTATING...

"...VERY, VERY FUCKING DEADLY."
I DID IT, Y'ALL! THE RAT QUEENS ARE DEAD!
ANNND THIS COURT IS FRIGGIN' ADJOURNED! HAH!

DAMN. THE RAT QUEENS NO MORE.
NEVER THOUGHT I'D SEE THE DAY.

HELL YEAH! TAKE IT IN, MY PEOPLE! TAKE. IT. IN.
TONIGHT WE CELEBRATE!

HEY, WATCH IT!
TAKE IT EASY!

LET THIS NOT BE A WARNING, BUT RATHER AN INVITATION TO A NEW WAY OF LIFE HERE IN NEW GARY.
LET'S BUILD EACH OTHER UP! LET'S NOT BE FRIGGIN' ASSHOLES!
LET'S--
AW COME ON!

YOU. THAT ARMY YOU =HUFF= GOT OUTSIDE CITY LIMITS? YEAH...YOU MIGHT WANNA =HUFF= GET A NEW ONE.

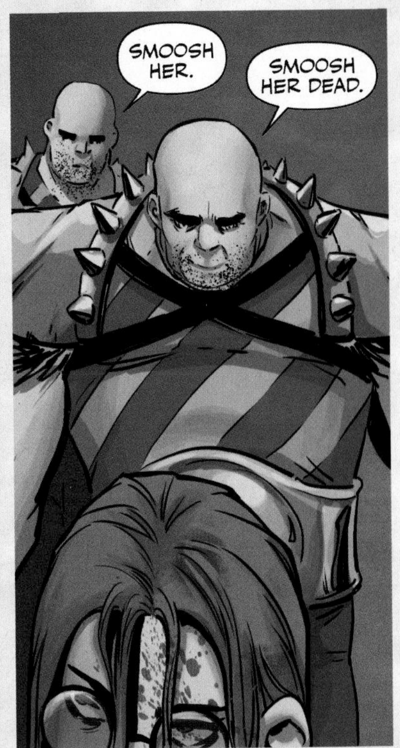
SMOOSH HER.
SMOOSH HER DEAD.

SHIK

YOU KILLED MY SISTERS. I'M GONNA MAKE YOU PAY. JUST LIKE I MADE YOUR ARMY.
OHHH NOOO... NONONO... PLEASE...

AUGHHHHHH!!!
...LET'S ADD ANOTHER SET OF BONES TO MY COLLECTION THEN, SHALL WE?

CHAPTER TWENTY

STINGS A LITTLE, DON'T IT? TRUST ME, THAT'S ONE-THOUSANDTH OF THE PAIN YOUR ILK HAS MADE ME FEEL.
BZZZZT
YOUR RAT QUEENS ARE *DEAD,* NERD. BUT I'VE STILL GOT AN ITCH TO SCRATCH.

GET YOUR POPPING CORNS, FOLKS! UNWRAP A NOUGAT OR TWO!
IT'S TIME FOR TONIGHT'S ENCORE. IT'S GOING TO BE A LONG ONE. *HEH.*

MADDIE?
SWEETIE, NO!

I'M... S-S-SORRY...

"...I COULDN'T--"

SAVE
THEM

OH. YOU. SO BRAVE AND VALIANT.
SO DRAMATIC.
WHERE AM I?
WELL, YOU'RE NOT DEAD. NOT LIKE THE OTHERS.
BUT I THOUGHT--
THAT YOU COULD JUST CEASE? LIKE THEM?
JUST BECAUSE YOU ARE BEHOLDEN TO THEIR LAWS OF CIVILITY, DOESN'T MEAN YOU CAN ESCAPE *WHAT* YOU ARE.

SO HERE YOU ARE. HERE'S WHERE IT'S BROUGHT YOU, AND HERE YOU WILL STAY.
BUT I CAN BRING THEM BACK...
≈SIGH≈ YOU'VE BEEN WARNED ENOUGH TIMES. I TIRE.

I IMAGINE YOU'LL SOON UNDERSTAND THAT I'VE BEEN TRYING TO HELP...
...AND THAT GODS WEREN'T MEANT TO HARBOR REGRET FOR THEIR ACTIONS.
SEE, THE CRUX OF UNDEFINABLE POWER...

...IS THAT MORE OFTEN THAN NOT, IT WILL LEAVE YOU POWERLESS.
YOU *CAN* DO WHAT YOU WANT. BUT OH, HOW YOU *SHOULDN'T.* I'VE TOLD YOU.

AND I'M NOT LISTENING. GODS STILL HAVE A CHOICE. *I HAVE* A CHOICE.
MMHM. YOU CHOSE *THEM,* DEE. YOU CHOSE *YOU.*

WH--WHAT HAPPENED?
WHERE--?
MMF
GODSPEED. YOU'RE ON YOUR OWN.

SUCKS BEING ON THE RECEIVING END, DON'T IT? *HUH?* FEELING GOOD ABOUT YOUR LIFE DECISIONS NOW?
WHAT LIFE DECISIONS, EVEN? YOU'RE, LIKE, EIGHT!
SHIT, IS SHE REALLY EIGHT...?

OWW-UHHH!
WHAT IN THE HELL--
SHRAK

DARK MAGIC. WHEN DID THAT BIRD-LOOKING GOAT-FUCKER LEARN DARK MAGIC?
I'LL HANDLE HIM.
FABULOUS-- I'M IN THE MOOD FOR *A LOT* OF STABBIN'.

WHAT?! THIS IS HORSE'S SHIT!
KILL THEM! KILL THEM KILL THEM KILL THEM! HACK THIS WHOLE DAMN CITY TO PIECES IF YOU HAVE TO!

GET TO MADDIE-- I'LL CARVE A PATH.
ON IT!
ASSES, NERDS-- SHOW 'EM!

HEY, MADDIE! WE WERE DEAD! TOTALLY NOT NOW THOUGH, SO DON'T WORRY. YOU OKAY?
A LITTLE CRISPY, BUT I THINK-- I THINK I'M OKAY.
GOOD, BECAUSE...
...NO NAPS FOR THE WICKED!
SHIK
THWAK
NGAH! WHY AM I ALWAYS BEING THROWN?!
JUST WHAT I THOUGHT--AN ARMY OF UNDER-ACHIEVERS.
SHIK
EVOKAR SHOCKARIUS!
BZZZZT
YOU JUST COULDN'T STAY DEAD, COULD YOU? COULDN'T DARE LET OTHER PEOPLE BE HAPPY.
YOU THINK PALISADE IS BETTER OFF WITH YOU?
I DID THIS CITY A FAVOR BY KILLING YOU. WE WERE THROWING A PARTY!
WHATEVER SHRED OF LIFE YOU HAVE LEFT INSIDE YOU--USE IT AGAINST US...
...AND IT'LL BE YOUR FUNERAL.
YOU HAVE NO IDEA WHAT'S INSIDE ME...FALSE GOD.
SHOOOOOM

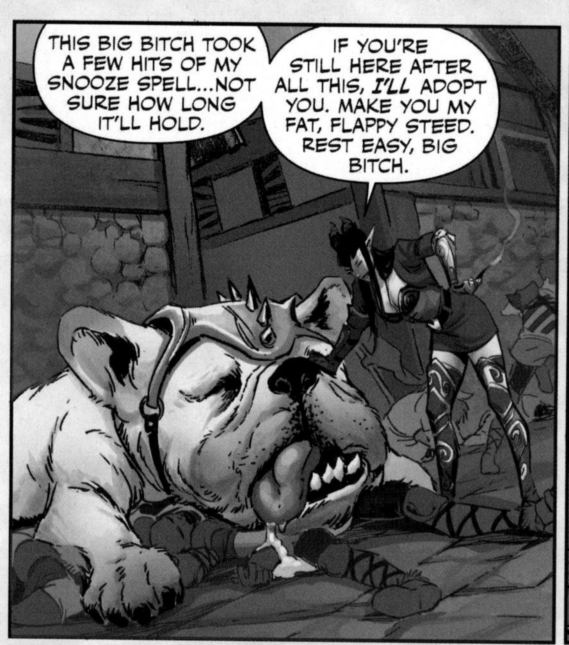
THIS BIG BITCH TOOK A FEW HITS OF MY SNOOZE SPELL...NOT SURE HOW LONG IT'LL HOLD.
IF YOU'RE STILL HERE AFTER ALL THIS, *I'LL* ADOPT YOU. MAKE YOU MY FAT, FLAPPY STEED. REST EASY, BIG BITCH.

DO WE HAVE TO FIGHT LIKE THIS ALL THE TIME?!
LOOK AT YOU--KILLING LIKE YOU'VE DONE IT YOUR WHOLE LIFE. I'VE NEVER BEEN MORE PROUD.
STAB

TERWILLIGER! YOU'RE ALIVE?
I'M PROUD TOO. OF YOU.
WASN'T REALLY DEAD. I DON'T *REALLY* EXIST, STUPID.
I'M *YOU*. ALWAYS HAVE BEEN. JUST THE ONE PART YA FORGOT.

WAIT! WHERE ARE YOU GOING?
SAME PLACE I'VE ALWAYS BEEN. DON'T YA LISTEN, YA BIG IDIOT?!
BUT... I'LL MISS YOU.
WELL STOP! YA GOT A SECOND CHANCE. YA DON'T *NEED* TO SEE ME ANYMORE.

"JUST LISTEN TO ME, FOR FUCK'S SAKE."

SHUNK
I HAD THE POWER ALL ALONG. WHO KNEW?
I'M DOING VERY WELL, EVERYONE!

I'M SO SORRY. I WON'T LEAVE YOU AGA--GOOD GODS, ARE YOU OKAY? YOU'RE COVERED IN BLOOD.
I'M SO PROUD OF YOU.
OH. Y-YEAH. I'M FINE. IT'S NOT MY BLOOD.

THAT'S ALL OF 'EM. I THINK A FEW ARE PLAYING DEAD THOUGH. YOU CAN TELL BY THE SMELL. THE *POO* SMELLS.
WELL, I FEEL FUCKIN' ***ALIVE.***
WE'RE NOT IN THE CLEAR JUST YET. LOOK.
HE'S HOLDING HIS OWN AGAINST A GOD?

I CAN DO THIS AS LONG AS IT TAKES, GARY. YIELD.
YOU'RE EMBARRASSING YOURSELF IN FRONT OF A FALLEN ARMY.
BZZZZT
HAHAHA. ***FUCK*** *A* ***GARY.***
YOU...

YOU... WERE...
...***WARNED.***

YOU'RE NOT GARY.

WHO ARE YOU?
H-HEH.

KSH

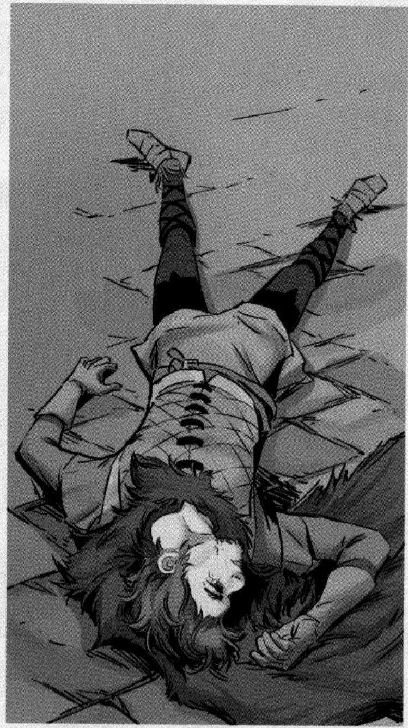

EVOKAR HEADSHOT. CUNT.

THANK YOU, HANNAH. I HAD IT THOUGH.
EH, LOTS OF FIREWORKS. NOT ENOUGH KILLING.
IF THE KING IS DEAD...
...MEANS THERE'S ROOM FOR A QUEEN.

ALL GOOD. HE'S DEAD, Y'ALL.
EVERYTHING'S BACK TO NORMAL NOW! WE DID IT! RAT QUEENS, BABY!

KOFF KAFF
ACK! IT'S THE UNDEAD! CUT ITS HEAD OFF, QUICK!

I FEEL...
I FEEL...
...HNNGUHH!

OHOHOH NO YOU DON'T.
EVOKAR--
HANG ON. WE NEED TO KNOW.

I THINK... I THINK I'M GONNA BARF.
SERIOUSLY. I'VE GOT THE WATERY BARF MOUTH. I CAN FEEL THE PUKE ON MY BREATH.
GODS, THAT'S THE WORST PART. THE BARF ANTICIPATION.

WHAT IN THE DANG HECK IS HAPPENING?
THIS ISN'T BLOREVION... WHERE AM I?
PALISADE?!

AHHH, NAW. NOT BUYING THE OL' DUHH, I DUNNO WHA' HAPPUNN ROUTINE.
WE'RE GONNA KILL YA, ASSHOLE.

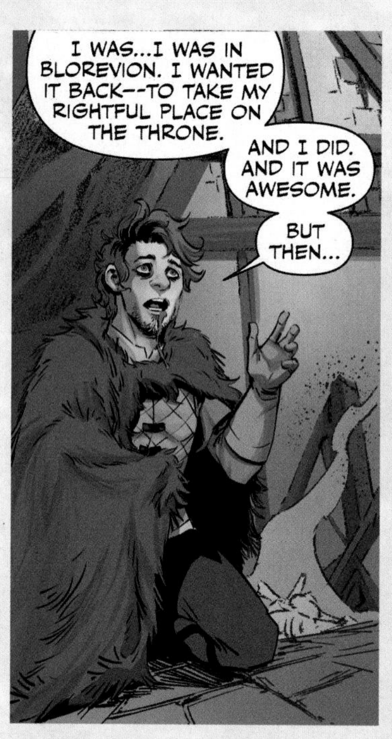
I WAS...I WAS IN BLOREVION. I WANTED IT BACK--TO TAKE MY RIGHTFUL PLACE ON THE THRONE.
AND I DID. AND IT WAS AWESOME.
BUT THEN...

...THEN THERE WAS A VOICE. IT SOUNDED COLD. IT LAUGHED AT ME.
IT CREEPED ONTO MY HEAD, FROM BEHIND. LIKE A HAND GRIPPING MY SKULL. THE FINGERS...

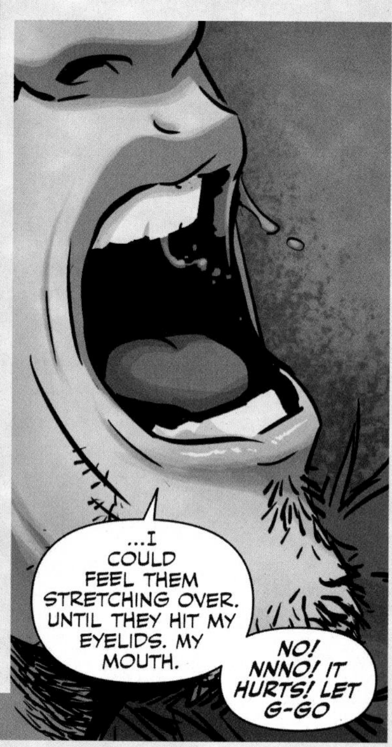
...I COULD FEEL THEM STRETCHING OVER. UNTIL THEY HIT MY EYELIDS. MY MOUTH.
NO! NNNO! IT HURTS! LET G-GO

BLURCH

WHAT THE FRICK?!

WHAT THE EVER-LOVING FRICK INDEED.

EVOKAR INCINERATE!
BZZZT
CRAAAK
WATCH FOR PUS!

CHOOOOM
AUGH!
GAHH!

OH MY GODS, IT'S GROWING...

MAYBE I SHOULD... AXE IT A QUESTION.
IT TOOK MY POWER AND JUST THREW IT RIGHT BACK AT US.
GARY! YOU DISGUSTING WORM-HOARDER, WHAT IN GODS' NAMES HAVE YOU BEEN EATING?

GRAPES! JUST...SO MANY HAND-FED GRAPES...I'M A KING!
WHAT GODSFORSAKEN KING'S GRAPES YOU GROWING IN THIS NIGHTMARE CITY?!

SHHH...
...THE GROWN-UPS ARE TALKING NOW. THIS DOESN'T CONCERN YOU.
IT'S YOU, ISN'T IT? THE VOICE THAT'S BEEN WARNING ME.

I HAVE TO ADMIT, I EXPECTED A LITTLE MORE.

HM? OH... THAT.
NO. THAT'S SOMEONE FAR MORE DIFFERENT THAN ME.
I'M GOING TO EXPLOIT YOUR DUMB-ASS DECISIONS, SURE, BUT UNLIKE THEM, I DON'T GIVE WARNINGS.

I LIKE TO WATCH, SEE? EVERY TINY LITTLE FUCKUP--EVERY WEE MISSTEP, I'M CHEERING YOU ON TO DIG A LITTLE DEEPER.
I DON'T CARE ABOUT THE BIG PICTURE. I CARE ABOUT MAKING YOU SUFFER.

WHEN THAT ASSHOLE GARY SHOWED A SHRED OF SELF-WORTH--SOMETHING YOU STRIPPED HIM OF, LIKE TRUE HEROES--I THOUGHT, OOH, THIS COULD BE FUN.
SO I GAVE HIM A LITTLE PUSH HERE. A LITTLE NUDGE THERE.

YOU HAVE NO IDEA HOW HILARIOUS IT'S BEEN TO WATCH YOU ALL GET PUNKED BY GARY THIS WHOLE TIME.

LIKE... GARY. C'MON, QUEENS.

SO, DEE, WE ALL EXPECTED A LITTLE MORE.

IT'S GONNA KILL HIM! I WANTED TO KILL HIM!
HO-HO-HOLD UP. I'VE NEVER SEEN DARK MAGIC LIKE THAT.

LOOK AT HOW GODS-DAMNED EASY IT COULD BE.
AN ORC. A MAGE. EVEN A GOD. AND YOU COULDN'T.

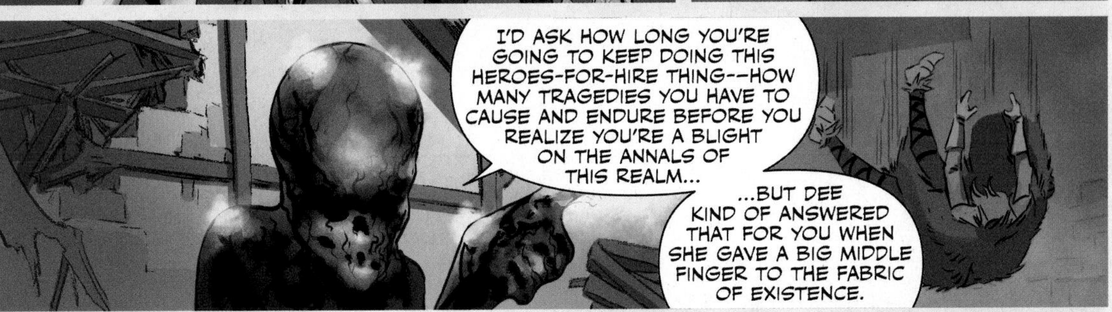
I'D ASK HOW LONG YOU'RE GOING TO KEEP DOING THIS HEROES-FOR-HIRE THING--HOW MANY TRAGEDIES YOU HAVE TO CAUSE AND ENDURE BEFORE YOU REALIZE YOU'RE A BLIGHT ON THE ANNALS OF THIS REALM...
...BUT DEE KIND OF ANSWERED THAT FOR YOU WHEN SHE GAVE A BIG MIDDLE FINGER TO THE FABRIC OF EXISTENCE.

WE'RE DONE FUCKING AROUND. WHAT DO YOU CARE WHAT HAPPENS TO US?
ARE YOU A TRICKSTER? IS THAT YOUUU, CASTIWYR?
IT'S TOYING WITH US. IT HAS BEEN THIS WHOLE TIME. IT WANTS TO SHOW US THE TRUTH--THAT'S THE POINT.

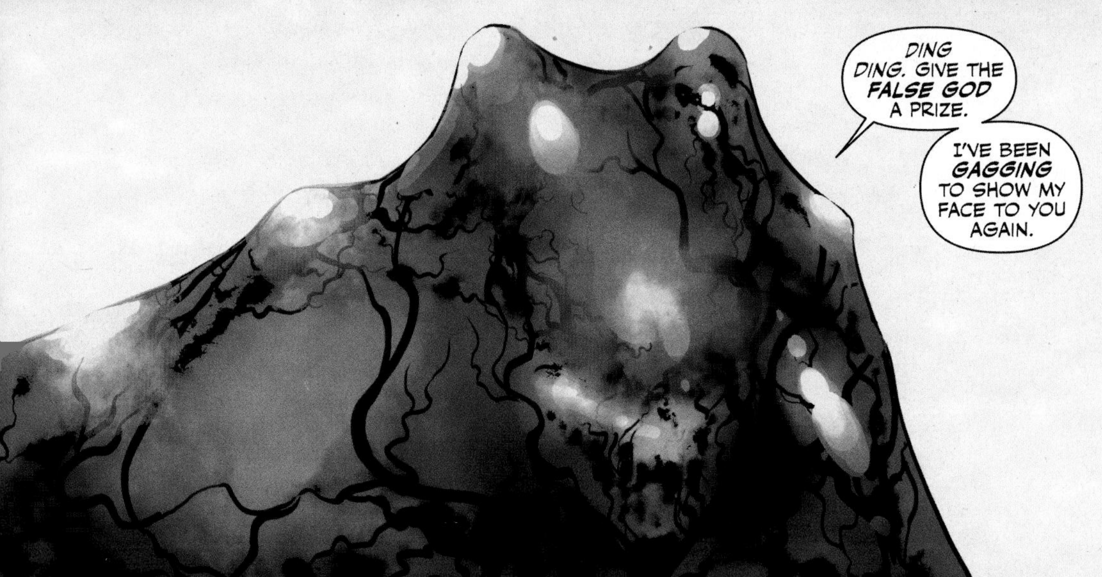
DING DING. GIVE THE ***FALSE GOD*** A PRIZE.
I'VE BEEN ***GAGGING*** TO SHOW MY FACE TO YOU AGAIN.

TA-FUCKING-DA.
WHILE IT KILLS ME THAT I CAN'T BE THE ONE TO KILL YOU, MY DEAR FUCKLINGS, I TAKE GREAT FUCKING PLEASURE IN KNOWING THAT YOUR SWEET DEATHS ARE IMMINENT AND INCOMING.
I'M GOING TO ENJOY MAKING WHAT'S LEFT OF YOUR PATHETIC LITTLE LIVES AN UTTER LIVING HELL BEFORE I KICK BACK AND WATCH EVERY LIVING THING GET SKULL-FUCKED INTO OBLIVION.
THIS ENTIRE REALM?
SO, SOOO FUCKED.

OH FUUUUUCK YOUUU!
I HATE EVIL ME. AND THAT'S SAYING A LOT SINCE I REALLY FUCKING LOATHE ME ME.

YOU'RE SICK. IF THE FLOODGATES OF APOCALYPSE REALLY ARE WIDE OPEN, AS YOU CLAIM, YOU JUST WANT TO KICK A WHOLE REALM WHILE IT'S DOWN?
PRETTY MUCH, UH HUH. I DO WHAT I PLEASE.

I WENT DEEEEP INSIDE MYSELF-- REGULAR HANNAH, YOU KNOW WHAT I'M TALKIN' ABOUT.
THOUGHT I COULD GO ON THE STRAIGHT AND NARROW. BE MY OWN PERSON... YEAHHH, NO.
IT'S JUST TOO EASY AND JUST TOO FUN TO BE ANYTHING OTHER THAN WHAT I AM.

SO YOU'RE A LOSER. JUST HANGING AROUND WITH NO FRIENDS AND NO ADVENTURE, WATCHING OTHERS SHOOT THEIR SHOTS.
REAL WINNER, EVIL ME. GOOD JOB.
OF COURSE YOUR PEA BRAIN DOESN'T GET IT. TIME IS ABSTRACT, BLAH BLAH BLAH. SUGAR, IT'S BEEN EONS SINCE I SAW YOU.

SEE, I DID CARVE MY OWN LITTLE REALM BETWEEN REALMS, BUT THESE FEET GET A LITTLE ITCHY, SO YOUR GAL'S GOTTA STRETCH.
I'VE BEEN TO THE NETHERVERSE, THE MACROVERSE, THE DARK, THE LIGHT, THE SILENCE, THE OVERWORLD, PLANET PAIN, THE COSMO-PLAINS...

...OF ALL THE SHIT I'VE SEEN AND THINGS I'VE SLAUGHTERED, NONE CURLED MY TOES QUITE LIKE YOUR TEARS.

ALL RIGHT, WE'VE HEARD ENOUGH.
YOU CAN DROWN IN OUR TEARS WHEN WE WEEP FOR JOY OVER YOUR MINGIN' CORPSE!

CRAAAK

HAH! THAT'S THE SPIRIT! WHATEVER MAKES YOU FEEL GOOD ABOUT YOURSELVES!
WOOOOOSH
WOOOOOM
BUT NOT TOO GOOD BITCHES.

WELP, I'M GONNA MAKE LIKE A BABY AND HEAD OUT, BEFORE YOU ALL START PISSING AND MOANING SOME MORE.
BE SEEING YOU AROUND, MY SALTY FUCK-RATS. ENJOY THE ONCOMING PLAGUES!

NO! EVIL HANNAH! STOP!
COWARDLY SKANK.

WELL FUCK. I'D SAY I'M SORRY...BUT... YEAH, THIS IS WEIRD.
NOT YOUR FAULT AT ALL, HANNAH. THAT ISN'T YOU. THAT'S A LUNATIC.
IS SHE LYING TO US?

OR IS THE END OF THE REALM REALLY COMING?

SO THEY SAY. I DON'T KNOW WHAT THAT MEANS YET, BUT I'M GOING TO FIND OUT EXACTLY WHAT I'VE STARTED.
LOOK. GARY AND HIS PALS ARE ON PARADE AGAIN.

THE SHIP...GET TO THE SHIP.
SET COURSE, FULL SAIL, FOR BLOREVION. I'D RATHER SLEEP IN THE ASHES OF A FALLEN KINGDOM THAN ENDURE ONE MORE NIGHT IN PALISADE...

HEY! THANKS FOR FUCKIN' THE WHOLE REALM FOR US ALL! THAT'S *BULL'S SHIT!*
YOU *SUCK* AND YOUR WHOLE CITY SUCKS *TOO.*

...AND SO HELP ME, GODS, MAY WE NEVER SEE THE RAT QUEENS EVER AGAIN.

Three Days Later

HARD TO BELIEVE JUST A FEW DAYS AGO WE WERE, *UHH*, ***DEAD***.
IT'S MORE A ***FEELING*** THAN ANYTHING. LIKE YOU'RE JUST ABOUT TO FALL ASLEEP. BUT THERE IS NO SLEEP. THERE'S NO AWAKE.
WHAT WAS THAT LIKE, ANYWAYS?
Sweet Tooth BAKERY

Sweet Tooth BAKERY
MADELINE OF GREAT CARNAGE--DEATH STALLION OF THE BATTLE OF GARY...
...AN OFFERING FOR YOU. A SURELY INSIGNIFICANT TOKEN OF OUR APPRECIATION FOR EVERYTHING YOU DID FOR PALISADE.

WOWZERS! IT'S THE GREAT RAT QUEENS!
PLEASE SIGN OUR SWORDS, PLEASE! YOU'RE MY FAVORITE OF ALL HISTORY!

I'VE NEVER SEEN PALISADE SO HAPPY. IT'S KIND OF--NO, IT'S SUPER WEIRD, ACTUALLY.
I KNOW, RIGHT? IT'S PEACEFUL. GOOD FOR THE SOUL, I SAY.
IT'S A LITTLE TOO QUIET, BETTS. BUT I WANT TO BELIEVE THIS IS THE START OF SOMETHING NEW.
I JUST CAN'T SHAKE THAT ***EVIL ME*** IS OUT THERE. WATCHING. WAITING.
WHAT IF THIS NEW BEGINNING IS JUST TOO GOOD TO BE TRUE? WHAT IF THIS ISN'T REAL?

"WHAT IF EVIL HANNAH'S RIGHT ABOUT WHAT'S COMING? WHAT IF WE HAVE COURTED SOMETHING TRULY HORRIBLE?"
"IF THE BEST OF TIMES ARE IN FACT HERE..."
PLEASE. SAY SOMETHING.
"...WHAT HAPPENS WHEN IT ALL COMES CRASHING DOWN HARDER?"
I'M NOT PROTESTING. I ACCEPT MY ACTIONS.
I ONLY ASK TO SEE THE FATE THAT I'VE BROUGHT MY WORLD.
AHH, DEE...THE ONLY LIVING GOD...
...YOU WILL.